Bound for Boothill

As Bert Cave came away from Boothill he swore vengeance on the cowmen of Faro Creek who had wrongly found his father guilty of stealing cattle, and murder, and then hanged him. The Cave property had been seized and Bert had only a meagre war-bag when his one true friend, Miriam Grosvenor, gave him weapons, bedroll and food, together with her prized horse.

He rode away to Billstown and was there befriended by a member of the Bryer gang of thieves and killers. Hardly had he been initiated into the gang than he was captured by ranchers who promised him hang-rope justice. Like father, like son, they said.

How could Bert save himself? Did anyone care? Could justice ever be done? He would go through hell before he found the answers to those questions.

By the same author

Terror Town

Bound for Boothill

Al Brady

A Black Horse Western

ROBERT HALE · LONDON

© 1955, 2003 Vic J. Hanson
First hardcover edition 2003
Originally published in paperback as
Guns of Hate by V. Joseph Hanson

ISBN 0 7090 7278 3

Robert Hale Limited
Clerkenwell House
Clerkenwell Green
London EC1R 0HT

Typeset by
Derek Doyle & Associates, Liverpool.
Printed and bound in Great Britain by
Antony Rowe Limited, Wiltshire

CHAPTER 1

Bert Cave turned only once. He took one last look at the knot of horsemen on the edge of the town, at the grove of cottonwoods by the creek, at the town itself, half-obscured by the heat-haze. His eyes travelled beyond, to something he could only visualise in his mind. The slopes of Boothill, the stunted brown grass, the huddle of pitiable little crosses among which the wind played endlessly.

He would remember Boothill far more clearly than he did the town. And, above all, he would remember the clump of cottonwoods by the gurgling creek. . . .

He was motionless for a moment of time and then he moved again.

His lean gangling figure was etched for a moment against the dying sun. Then, finally he passed out of sight of the men watching, and they turned their horses and rode back into town.

Bert walked on with long gangling strides, his meagre war-bag swinging in his right hand. He wore faded Levis, a threadbare check shirt and a moth-eaten sheepskin coat. He wobbled on the scuffed heels of his riding boots like a man unused to walking, a man in fact who was far more at home on a horse. But he was not even a man yet, though there was already an ageless sorrow clouding the dark eyes in the smooth brown face beneath the battered sweat-stained slouch hat.

His free hand was hooked in his belt. But there was no gun-belt there, not even a knife, only a battered water-canteen. He was a youth of nineteen odd summers – without a horse and without a weapon. A very sad state to be in, particularly in the lawless West at this time.

He reached the narrow road which led out of town, which ran for thirty-odd miles through scrubland, desert and small hills to the next settlement. He walked on the verge to avoid raising a dust. He kept close to cover too, whenever it was available. He trusted no man, and would not do so for a very long time yet.

But a woman was different, particularly if – like himself – she was not yet quite grown-up. His eyes lit a little as she came out of the rocks at the side of the trail.

'I couldn't let you go like this, Bert—'

'But, Miriam, your father!'

'He thinks I'm at the Caldicotts. Here.' She beckoned to him.

He followed her behind the rocks. There her own horse stood, and one for him too, the horse he had always admired the most when he had been welcome at her father's ranch.

She handed him a gunbelt, complete with a Colt .45. She showed him the rifle in the saddle scabbard, and the bedroll and the new war-bag packed with eats.

For a moment he was inarticulate and could only look at her. Then he said quietly, 'I can't take him, Miriam. Your father would be furious when he found out.'

'I'm not scared of his fury,' said the girl. 'I'm the apple of his eye, you know that. I must prove to him that I still believe in you, Bert – I must. . . .'

He was no proof against her woman's powers of persuasion, and finally mounted the horse. 'I'll bring him back some day, Miriam,' he said huskily.

A glance passed between them. It was all that was needed. But the girl added: 'Sure you will, Bert. I know you will. . . .'

And she went on even further, which perhaps she should not have done: 'Please don't do anything foolish, Bert.'

He did not say anything, but his face stiffened a little, and his eyes were hooded from her once more. It was so easy for her to caution him that way, she the pampered daughter of a rich widower rancher, protected no matter which way she turned.

She seemed to realize she had said a little too much and was silent as she rode on with him. He, in his turn, relented. After all, she had risked something in coming out to him like this. The men from the town might have still been following him. They would not have hesitated in making things uncomfortable for her, of fanning her father's wrath to a pitch even greater than that which was already inevitable. He was tempted once more to relinquish her offering. But he had already given his word, so he stayed put in the saddle.

Women were funny creatures!

From now on he would have no time for women. His life would be dedicated to one thing, and one thing only.

He gave Miriam a sidelong glance. Suddenly he looked at her in a way he had never looked at her before – and he was startled by what he saw.

She was no longer the stubby tomboy of his boyhood. She had grown into a beautiful young woman. Thinking of his boyhood brought back other memories – which gave him pain. But she spoke then, shaking him from his reverie.

'I must leave you here, Bert.' She halted her horse, turned in the saddle and held out her hand.

The hand was small but her grip was firm and mannish. Her whispered, 'Good luck, *amigo*', echoed in his mind as he rode on.

He would be back. They both knew it somehow.

It was night when he reached Billstown, and the dwelling-places on the edge of it were all in darkness. But the saloons and dives in the main street were still jumping. He remembered Billstown as a place that never really shut up shop. It was much smaller than Faro Creek, the place in which he had spent so much of his short life, the place he had recently left. But it had more colour and life and, in his present mood he was drawn to it like a moth to a flame.

Faro Creek was permanent now in all the squalor of its slums, all the showy and gimcrack respectability (the slugs beneath the pretty stone) of its more palatial establishments. It had been there a long time and could spread no further now, for it was ringed by the rangelands of the people who were its bosses, Miriam's father amongst them. But Billstown was in the heart of the Arizona badlands, a refuge of outlaws and unscrupulous people in search of a good time. Its population fluctuated and so did its buildings. From time to time one or two of them were mysteriously burned down. Twice in Bert's memory there had been major conflagrations but the town always grew again, lustier than ever. It was flattened in one place; forthwith it spread in another.

Billstown had its bosses too, or its would-be bosses. They came and went like leaves in a storm. Sometimes they stayed, never to move any more. Despite its size, Billstown had a far larger Boothill than Faro Creek.

As Bert rode down the dusty cart-rutted main street he reflected wryly that it was fitting he should end up here in Billstown. Was not it where folks had expected him to end up anyway?

He turned his horse in, tied it to a hitch-rail. He looked up into the naptha flares which gave a gay glare to the front of the saloon as if he expected to find some answers to things there. But what he sought was inside, so he entered.

He was assailed on all sides by noise. Cigarette smoke stung his eyes and nostrils. He jostled his way through the crowd towards the bar. A painted

woman caught his arm, called him a 'nice boy'. He
shook her off brusquely. Men and women, huddled
close together, were shuffling in travesties of the
dance. Other couples made love openly in corners.
Games of other kinds were also in session. Croupiers
intoned the odds. Poker-players squinted tensely
through the smoke. In a corner by the bar a pianist,
squeeze-box player and guitarist endeavoured to
make music.

The bar consisted of a huge slab of pine placed
across empty liquor barrels. The latter, long since
empty, were liberally peppered with bullet-holes.
Behind them a big man in a white apron presided.
Bert was brought up short by the sight of him, a
stranger. And a stranger who was looking at the new
arrival rather suspiciously. He bellied up to the bar.

'What can I do for you, kid?' said the big man.

'Rye.'

'Rye it is.' He filled the glass, passed it across, took
the money, made change. And all the time he was
watching the customer with his little piggy eyes.

The young man took a swallow of the rye and
blinked. Then he said casually: 'Is Mike Loper
around?'

'Whadyuh want him for, kid?'

'He's an old friend of my father's. The old man
asked me to look him up if I happened this way.'

'Oh,' said the big man. Then he grinned, showing
brown snaggle-teeth. 'You came to the wrong place,
kid. If you want to see Mike you gotta walk further on
along the street and climb the hill.' The grin
widened. 'Even then I ain't promising you'll see him.'

Bert quelled his irritation and the fear that was beginning to niggle at the back of his mind. 'Mike used to own this place, didn't he?'

'Oh, sure. But not any more. All Mike owns now are a few square feet of Boothill.'

It was as if he had strode round his bar and kicked the young man in the stomach. But he was not quite as heartless as he seemed. 'Jeepers, younker!' he exclaimed. 'You look all tuckered out. C'mon around back here an' sit down.'

Bert took the stool behind the bar, and another drink to go with it. It had seemed that Mike Loper was the only friend he had left in the world, except Miriam, and she did not count now because she was among his enemies. The news of Mike's death had seemed to knock the bottom out of his world. But now he was getting back his sense of proportion; the sudden surprising sympathy of the big barman helped in this immeasurably.

He would have to thank the big man for other things – or curse him to eternity – before the night was out.

After a while he asked the manner of Mike Loper's death.

The barman said: 'He ran foul of the boss.'

'The boss?'

'Yeh. Con Bryer.'

The rather unusual-sounding name – so unusual that Bert wondered for a moment whether 'Con' was female – struck a chord in his mind. But he could not put his finger on the reason for this; and the big man was talking again, he seemed very keen to talk about 'the boss'.

11

'Con used to run a gambling joint in 'Frisco but had to come out here for his health. He's better now, but he liked it out here so figured he'd stay.' The barman chuckled. 'Who wouldn't with pickings like this.' He waved a big hand to encompass the teeming room. 'I came out with him in the first place – I was his right-hand man in 'Frisco – an' we picked up Jack Tremaine on the way, so tuh speak. . . .'

The chord was struck again, and this time Bert had no doubts. 'Jack Tremaine, the gunfighter?' he put in.

'The same, kid. He's the boss's half-brother. They were both raised out here. I guess Con never really got the West out of his blood – he was bound to finish up back here sooner or later. I'm a Westerner myself too, really. I was raised in the Panhandle. Ever been to the Panhandle, son?'

'No.' Bert wished the big man would stick to the point. He wanted to hear more about Con Bryer, and the fabulous Jack Tremaine.

'Greatest country on earth,' said the barman, no doubt still referring to the Panhandle. Then he was called away to serve drinks, leaving Bert to fume alone for a while.

The big man finally returned: 'I had a kid brother somep'n like you back in the old days,' he said. 'He was killed by Injuns.'

Bert made an appropriately regretful sound. He realized now why the sentimental big man had taken to him so quickly; but he could not help wondering whether the barman had forgotten his original theme.

But he had not, it seemed. In fact, he absolutely plunged back into it.

'When Con an' Jack an' me rode into Billstown, Mike Loper was boss here. This place was his head-quarters. We came in here. Mike himself was sitting in a game of poker with two of his boys, and a sucker they had picked up from someplace. Con is what you might call a born gambler, it's meat an' drink to him. He was drawn to this game like a hound-dawg to a beef stew. One of Mike's boys stepped out an' Con asked if he could take his place. It was a calculated move, I guess. I've figured all along that Con might've been after something more than just a few hands of poker!'

The big man made a dramatic pause. Fate conspired with him and a voice bawled: 'Hey, Bucky,' and he turned back to the bar.

'Bucky'. The name suited him somehow. Bert waited impatiently for what else Bucky would tell him.

And presently Bucky returned and the story was told. It was not a new one. As simple and elemental as the brutal ways of the West. Con, a wizard with cards, soon began to win. His presence mysteriously changed the sucker's luck too, and pretty soon, between them, they had cleared the board.

Then Mike Loper sprang to his feet, accused Con of cheating and went for his gun. Con beat him to the draw and shot him between the eyes. One of his henchmen who tried to plug Con in the back was killed by Jack Tremaine.

Bucky spread his huge hands. 'That night

13

Billstown got itself a new boss – just like that. Mike had a silent partner or somep'n. Con bought him out, sent him packing. We took over.'

Bucky was called away again, but he had obviously finished, anyway. Bert reflected that the big man's obvious regard for Con and Jack had prejudiced him in their favour. But he knew that Mike Loper had not been particularly scrupulous – he had always said he wanted to die standing up – and could be most of the tale, if not all of it, was quite true.

Bert felt suddenly weary, so when Bucky returned, the youth said: 'Thanks for everything, suh. I'm kinda tired. I think I'll go bed down my horse an' find a kip for myself too.'

'Try Ma Prentiss jest down the street,' said the barman with a jerk of his thumb.

'Thanks – Bucky.'

'You ain't told me your name yet, son,' said Bucky with gentle rebuke.

'Bert Cave.'

'Bert Cave, huh! Goodnight, Bert.'

'Goodnight.'

Suddenly Bucky did not seem quite so benign, though Bert could not think why. Maybe his weary lightheadedness was making him imagine things.

The night air cleared his head a little. He made his way to Ma Prentiss's, a sagging frame establishment. Ma was big, rawboned and of sixty odd summers. She had the face of a gargoyle and the profane tongue of a mule-driver. She stood no nonsense, and even the toughest – and they didn't come any tougher than in Billstown – respected her. She found Bert a small room in the eaves. She looked him over keenly, but asked no questions.

The livery stable was conveniently near. Bert left his horse there to the care of a Mexican boy and went back to Ma's and a lumpy pallet which felt to him like a parcel of clouds.

CHAPTER 2

A strident voice awakened him. His hand reached instinctively for the gun under his pillow. A hand held a lantern aloft and he recognized Ma. 'The livery stable's on fire!' she yelled. 'I want every man out to fight it before it reaches this place.'

Bert thought immediately of his horse. As Ma thudded from the room he leapt from the bed. A few moments later, clad in trousers, shirt and boots, he was clattering down the stairs with other boarders.

The stable was doomed. The Mexican boy staggered out, coughing and spluttering. Bert grabbed him, shook him, teeth gleaming in the red light, eyes glaring. 'The horses! The horses!'

'I let 'em loose – out the back way!'

Bert, instantly contrite, yelled an apology at the boy and ran up the alley beside the stables. The heat made him flinch; he protected one side of his face with his hands as he ran. Then he was out in the open again.

A squealing horse ran past him, but he saw clearly that it was not his own. He turned the corner fully. He

17

saw a man running, saw him leap, catch hold of another crazed beast, leap on to its back. This second horse was Bert's own. He yelled and the man turned his head, but instead of stopping the horse, kicked it to greater speed. Only then did Bert realize that here was a skunk of a horse-thief, taking advantage of the fire. Could be, even, that he had started the fire with that purpose in mind. He had an eye for good horseflesh: the one he rode now was surely the pick of the bunch – and Bert didn't mean to lose it either if he could possibly help it. He drew the gun he had automatically slipped into the waistband of his trousers before he left Ma's place. He yelled again, but the rider paid no heed. He was rapidly drawing away from the aura of firelight. Bert raised the gun, took aim, fired.

He felt a little sick as he saw the body fall to the dust. Nobody would blame him for shooting down a pesky horsethief, surely the lowest type of sneak known to the West. Still, he had hated doing it. It was the first time he had actually shot a man; he had never even considered himself a good shot. He pouched the gun, ran forward.

He called again, more gently, to the horse, and the beast, obviously recognizing his voice, slowed down. The man staggered to his feet. Bert was relieved to find that he hadn't killed anybody after all.

Then, as Bert got nearer, the other man turned at bay, going for his gun. Bert could never have beaten that draw. He leapt, fist swinging. The blow caught the horse-thief on the side of the head. His gun spun from his hand, and for the second time he hit the dust.

He seemed to be made of india-rubber. He scrabbled for the gun. Bert fell on him, and they threshed in a tangle of arms and legs for a moment, then the man underneath began to weaken. Bert felt a stickiness on his fingers and realized the thief had been wounded after all. The gun was out of harm's way by now. Bert grabbed the man by the shoulders and began to lift him.

But he dropped him quickly enough when the voice spoke from behind.

'Straighten up, friend. Reach for the clouds.'

Bert did as he was told. His erstwhile opponent moaned in the dust.

'What's going on?' said the newcomer.

Bert threw the reply back over his shoulder. 'This buzzard tried to steal my horse. I ain't so sure it wasn't him who started the fire, either.'

'Up to your old tricks again, huh, Lenny?'

Lenny squirmed in the dust. 'I was trying to save the horse,' he whined. 'This hotheaded young cuss didn't give me time to explain anything. He throwed down on me. He got me in the arm.'

'A flea-bite evidently,' said the voice sardonically. 'You were giving a pretty good account of yourself with both arms when I came along. Get up!'

Lenny climbed complainingly to his feet. Bert began to turn and was stopped in his tracks when the voice snarled: 'Keep still younker. This gun's on a hair-trigger. Get up alongside him, Lenny, an' no funny tricks.'

'I ain't aiming to commit suicide, Jack,' said the wounded hero ingratiatingly.

The name 'Jack' had an impact on Bert that froze his blood. Did that sardonic voice belong to Jack Tremaine, killer? It could be another Jack, of course, but Bert was glad he had not turned quickly in an effort to find out. The effort might have cost him his life.

'March – both of yuh,' said the voice.

They did as they were told, keeping pointedly apart. Bert heard the slow clop-clop of a horse's hooves and realized 'Jack' was leading his (Bert's) mount.

Jack directed them into an alley which Bert figured probably led alongside the saloon. He halted them outside a door from beneath which escaped a tiny thread of light. With a suddenness that startled Bert, Jack shouted: 'Open up!'

The door swung open almost immediately. 'Keep marching,' snapped Jack.

Blinking in the light the two men entered the room. Jack followed them, kicked the door to behind him. The room was almost bare, except for a huge desk and two or three chairs, but what was there looked good and there was that unheard of luxury, a carpet on the floor. There were four men in the room, apart from the newcomers. Everybody was standing.

For a moment of time there was silence. Then Bert spotted Bucky and greeted the barman warily.

'Howdy, Bert,' said the big man. 'You certainly get around.'

The man directly before the desk spoke then. 'Who's this?' he asked in a soft, even voice.

'It's the kid I told you about, Con,' said Bucky. Everybody waited for the other man to speak again. He was so obviously the boss. Bert had a chance to take a good look at big-shot gambler, Con Bryer.

He saw a slim man of medium height with a strong, hatchet face, cold eyes, full sensual lips unadorned by the fungus his kind usually sported. Bert had an idea somehow that this man was, in fact, a little above 'his kind'. Con wore the usual get-up, though maybe that even was a little better-class than was usual.

Iron-grey coat with velvet braid, a fancy waistcoat that was not too flashy, striped pipestem trousers, string tie. He was hatless and his hair was long, thick, black and beautifully groomed. He had no weapons in sight.

'I guess you'll know me again, younker,' he said. There was a hint of humour in his voice, but his eyes remained cold. Then before Bert could say anything, the gambler went on: 'Maybe you better speak your piece now, Jack.'

Bootheels were sibilant on the carpet. Bert had no doubt now that his captor was Jack Tremaine, so he took a good look at the man when he came into view. At first he was surprised. He was also rather disappointed in what he saw.

The fabulous Jack Tremaine was a wizened young-old little man who walked with a slight limp. What Bert could see of his face was not very prepossessing either, and the hair that showed beneath the sweat-stained slouch hat was of a dirty-grey colour.

He listened to what Jack said in that sardonic,

21

almost toneless voice of his. Then he could not resist breaking in himself, telling everybody what he had already told Jack outside. The gunman did not contradict him. The horse-thief, Lenny, started to speak and was told curtly to shut up by Con.

'The next time you play tricks without orders, Lenny, it'll be your last. This is your last warning.'

'I'm sorry, boss. I saw this horse an' I—'

'I know what you thought. Did you start that fire?'

'No, boss. On my honour! I felt kinda groggy an' I was walkin' an'—'

'All right, all right. Get over in the corner and let Med fix that arm for you.'

Lenny went over into the corner and was joined by a frail, elderly man with a beard. Con turned his attention to Bert once more. 'You certainly stopped Lenny pretty tidily, kid.'

He smiled, and the smile lit his hatchet face and even his eyes. Suddenly, Bert took a strange liking to him.

He remembered that this was the man who had killed Mike Loper and that he should be hating him. But he had felt a lot of hate, and at the moment he lost most of it and grinned at Con Bryer as if they were conspirators. It was the first time he had grinned for a long time, and it gave him a good feeling.

Con told him to sit down, and he did so. He suddenly remembered his horse and asked about him. Bucky winked and said he'd go see to the beast. Con said: 'Bucky's told me a bit about you, but not much. Why did you come to Billstown looking for

Mike Loper? What did you expect Mike to do for you?'

All the hate came back then, though it was not directed at Con. All the horror, the grief, the terrible frustration. It was good to talk about it to somebody who seemed to understand.

Con listened to the very end then quietly made his proposition.

It did not shock Bert. Nothing, he thought, would ever shock him anymore. He fell in with the proposition right away.

Bucky returned, saying that Bert's mount (a mighty clever piece of horseflesh!) had already found its way to the saloon's own stable. He was the first to congratulate and welcome 'the Kid' as he called Bert. Then the younker was introduced to the rest of the men in the room.

'Medico' Jones, 'Med' for short. Frail, elderly, diffident in manner, with a straggly grey beard that might once have been a smart and dashing Buff'ler Bill Cody-imperial. Candy Sampson, little older than Bert himself, but a mean hardcase from the top of his close-cropped dark head to the heels of his slovenly cowboots. His greeting was perfunctory and he eyed the newcomer with something like contempt. Jack Tremaine – for the first time Bert got a look at the notorious gunman full-face. There was all the evil of the ages in that face and not a little of its sadness too. The eyes had an abysmal look; they were colourless, featureless marbles. But Jack greeted the Kid not unkindly, and the grip of his lean, sinewy hand was warm and firm. Even the wounded Lenny shook hands, though with patent ill-grace.

'You'll meet the rest of the boys later on,' said Con Bryer. He looked about him. 'Conference is over for tonight, boys.' He turned again to Bert with another of his lightning changes of tone, from velvet glove to rock fist and back again. 'You can have a room in the place. The one next to Jack's is empty.'

'I'll have to get my stuff from Ma's,' said Bert.

'That'll be taken care of,' said Con. 'Go with Jack.'

'Follow me, Kid,' said the gunfighter, and Bert, who, to tell the truth, was deadly tired, did as he was told. Probably Con would see that Ma got paid for one half of a night's lodgings too. He looked like the kind of man who would take care of everything. Bert was glad of somebody who, it seemed, would guard him from worry for a while.

He followed Jack along the passage to the barroom, a depressing sight in its empty havoc. The others were close behind them. Bucky called goodnight and so did Med, but Candy and Lenny did not speak. Up the stairs they went and along a well-carpeted landing. They passed a few doors and then Jack halted almost at the end of the landing.

'This is yours.' He jerked a thumb. 'I'm right next door. You'll find everything you want in there. If there's anything you want partic'ler just holler, but don't leave it too late or I might jump outa bed a-shooting.'

'I'll be all right. Thanks, Mr Tremaine.'

'Jack's the name, Kid. We're gonna be saddle-buddies a long time – if you keep in line.'

'Goodnight – Jack.'

'Goodnight.'

The gunman limped away, his wizened figure throwing grotesque shadows on the walls.

Entering the room, Bert was surprised to notice that almost half of the door was taken up by a glass panel, though it was covered with net curtain on the inside. He had never seen a door like that before. Still, he hadn't been around much; maybe this was a new-fangled Eastern idea. Con looked like the kind of character who would go for new-fangled ideas. He had come from 'Frisco, anyway, and Bert had heard that some of the new-fangled contraptions there had to be seen to be believed.

He found the lamp and lit it and looked around the room. Compared to the room he had left at Ma's, or even back in what had used to be his home, this was the acme of luxury. But he was too tired to take it in all at once. All he wanted right then was to sleep – to sleep a week. He shucked off his clothes and got into the comfortable bed. Then he leaned out to turn off the lamp.

Half between sleeping and waking, he thought he saw a shadow on the panel of the door. An ominous shadow. But it was gone in a second, like part of a fleeting dream, and when Bert awoke, the sun was streaming through the curtains at the window and it was a new day.

It was a day he would always remember, the day he entered into a new profession, a profession that only a few short weeks ago he would not have dreamed of entering. But that had been before the hate entered into his soul – the iron. This was his chance –

perhaps his only chance to do, ultimately, what he had sworn to do. He entered into man's estate now: already a man beyond his years, and when the unlicked look was purged from him, a fitting companion for Jack Tremaine, Candy Sampson, and the rest.

That day he was taken out to the hide-out to meet the rest. After that it was too late to turn back, even if he had wanted to. 'If you keep in line', Jack Tremaine had said; and Jack knew what he was talking about!

CHAPTER 3

They rode in the driving rain and the thunder. Once they stopped to get their bearings, and it was Bert Cave, the Kid, who gave it to them. This was one of the nights he had been waiting for.

They rode on and he was well in the forefront, with Jack and Con and Candy Sampson, who would not let this fresh Kid outdo him in anything and nursed a smouldering resentment all the time.

They heard the sound of the cattle and stopped again, listening. The wind played ominous tricks, but finally Con gave the word again and they went on, increasing their speed.

The wind buffeted at them, shrieked past their ears. Then Con waved his hand aloft and forward in a sweeping motion, and they veered slowly. And finally the wind was behind them, driving them on like demons.

Jack Tremaine, action incarnate on his magnificent horse, the pain of his gammy hip (smashed by a bullet years ago) forgotten entirely in his savage joy of the ride and what lay at the end of it. Con Bryer, a strange man, as much at home on a horse as at a gambling table or a banquet at a governor's mansion, every inch a leader. Candy Sampson, spawn of a mining camp dance-hall girl and an unknown roustabout, nurtured in evil and violence and sudden death – he had never known another life and he didn't want another one. 'Med' Jones, father of the damned, doctor of the ills of the damned; drunk, as he usually was on these rides. How could he ride without that, he who had a degree from a famous college and the corroding, malignant memory of a terrible failure?

Scarfaced Tim Baggs from Laredo, wanted by the law of five different States. Lenny, the horse-thief, drunk too, because he would be scared if he wasn't: he was the finest wrangler a man could find, invaluable in that way; Con's boys only rode the finest horseflesh, and it was Lenny's job to look after them. Grado Bear, half-Indian, taciturn and deadly. Bruiser Pink, bare-knuckle fighter from the Barbary Coast, a mountain of a man with a pinpoint brain. And the others, the motley crew, merciless, deadly, as ravening as the storm through which they rode like fiends out of hell.

And fiends they must have seemed as they swept down on the restless herd and the luckless night-riders who strived to keep it in check.

Until the last moment the hoofbeats of the racing horses were muffled by the blustering of the elements. That night cruel Mother Nature was on the side of evil. The heavens were suddenly split apart by jagged gashes of lightning, which spotlighted fitfully the dark riders, so that they might have been part of the storm, so that the heart of the first man who saw them was clutched momentarily by superstition. By the time he had realized what was really happening it was too late: his cry was drowned by the thunder, his gun was only half out of its holster when a bullet slammed into his chest. Then he was spotlighted by the flash of lightning, clawing desperately at the lowering skies, then being whipped away as if by a giant hand, to disappear finally beneath the threshing hooves of his own half-crazy horse. The beast smelled death. These strange creatures of the night were death; she bolted before them.

Her terror was communicated to the herd, and the next moment the riders had a stampede on their hands.

The thunder of the hooves rose to a hammering crescendo, drowning even the cacaphony of the storm. The men rode fast, but helplessly, their shooting and shouting was like spitting in the wind. They could only keep out of harm's way and strive to keep pace with the maddened beasts, hoping that eventually they would run themselves out.

Con Bryer rode like a maniac and it was he who spotted, in a lightning flash, more riders coming towards them. He realized his own men were outnumbered by two to one. There was only one thing to do. He wheeled his horse and gave the signal to head for home. The newcomers did not chase them far, but began to concentrate on the cattle. Unless something was done quickly by every man available, the herd would be to hell and gone by morning.

The Bryer gang were a pretty silent bunch when they got back to Billstown. Bucky was surprised to see them back so soon, but wisely asked no questions until they had cooled off. Con immediately went upstairs to the consolations of his current light o' love. Candy Sampson had a flesh wound in his arm, which was quickly treated by Med Jones. Otherwise, the boys were unscathed, only wet and dirty and tired and very, very disgruntled.

Bert Cave's first ride with the gang had turned into a farce. Though a pretty terrible kind of farce when you stopped to think about it. He could still see that first night-rider and the way he had disappeared beneath the churning hooves of his own horse. Bert had known the man.

Bert Cave's hate had turned to bile in his mouth. Although maybe that was just because of the way things had turned out in the finish, all these half-drowned rats around him looked kind of bilious.

It was as if Bucky read the younker's thoughts. 'Never mind, Kid,' he grinned. 'It'll be better the second time.'

'If he doesn't jinx us again,' said the wounded Candy viciously.

Bert turned on him. 'Talk sense,' he snarled, his own hate crystallising now he had somebody near at which to aim at. 'I didn't start the storm, did I? Or the stampede? Or the bunch who sent us a-running with our tails between our legs?'

Candy rose, glaring at Bert, then glancing slyly

around him. 'Did yuh hear what he said, boys? Our tails between our legs. He thinks we're yellow.'

Nobody took this up. This enraged Candy further. 'Nobody calls me yellow an' gets away with it,' he snarled. He turned fully towards Bert and half-crouched, his right hand – the good one – poised over the butt of his gun. But he did not draw.

A voice said: 'If one of you goes for his gun, you both die. I promise this!'

There was only one man who could promise this. And keep his promise too. He stood negligently with his thumbs hooked into his belt and a cigarette drooping from his lower lip. He was wizened and very unspectacular-appearing. But there was death in his eyes.

Candy's malignant eyes widened in their turn, and it seemed as if he would disregard the warning, as if he would try something, go down shooting like a madman.

The killer's trance had been upon him, but suddenly it was gone, and it was as if somebody had kicked him in the guts. He licked dry lips. It was Bucky who saved his face by saying cheerfully: 'Jack's in command when the boss ain't here. You two younkers had better bide by what he says unless you want to get hurt permanently. Besides, Con wouldn't like that. He'd be liable to dock your pay or somep'n.'

He guffawed. Med Jones giggled nervously. Lenny the wrangler joined in sycophantically. The tension was broken.

'I'll go get some hot coffee an' a leetle of somep'n

31

stronger,' said Bucky, and, still chortling, went out.

Suddenly Jack Tremaine spoke again. Everybody turned towards him to get his words clearly. But it was to Bert and Candy that they were aimed.

'Con don't like bad feeling between his boys. You know that, Candy, and you, Kid; I'm telling you right now. To fight among ourselves is just plumb foolishness. It's also a danger to the gang as a whole and can't be allowed.'

His voice was soft now, conversational. It hardly seemed credible that only a few seconds ago he had threatened to kill the two people to whom he now spoke. Bert Cave felt a shiver go through him. What kind of man was this?

Jack was going on: 'I don't know what has caused the friction between you two young cusses, but it's got to be settled once an' for all. We can't afford wasteful gunplay' – a hint of sardonic humour here – 'so we'll use the other way. A nice little private mill, just the two of you with only us boys watching, out someplace where there ain't any snoopers.'

'I cain't fight with this gammy arm,' said Candy sullenly.

'I know it,' Jack told him. 'But it's only a scratch and will soon get better. Then you'll fight.'

'Suits me,' said Candy, grinning evilly at Bert.

The latter said: 'I'll be glad to accommodate yuh.'

'And whoever wins or don't win, that'll be the end of it,' rapped Jack. 'The next one who steps outa line I'll attend to personally.'

'I ain't got the time for prizefighting either,' he added with deadly meaning.

Nobody argued with him, least of all the two young men who were the sudden target for his malice.

Bucky put in an appearance again, carrying a tray full of cheering liquids.

Bert Cave had been filled with savage anticipation for this night. This had been his first chance to get back at his enemies, the powerful ones of Faro Creek, the enemies of his father. This had been his first chance to fight them, as he saw it, with their own weapon – brute force. Within the law or without the law, that made no difference. He just could not see any difference nowadays; the law had not helped his father.

There was no law in Faro Creek except the law of the powerful ones. The only difference that he could see between Faro Creek and Billstown was that 'the Creek' disguised its black heart behind a facade of respectability and self-righteousness, whereas Billstown almost flaunted its wickedness.

It was very late when he went to bed, but he was up again just after dawn. He went out into the pearly slumbering morning and got his horse. He had an idea that Con wouldn't like him riding out alone like this so soon after a job. But he could not think of even Con as his master yet, so out he went.

The breeze was sweet, swishing the grass around his horse's fetlocks. His mind was still a little tangled up and he was trying to straighten it out. But pretty soon the balmy peace of the morning stole into his soul and he gave himself up entirely to the enjoyment of it. He let his horse take him where he would. The beast jogged along peacefully, taking him further away from Billstown, the events of last night, the terrible happenings before that. He might have just been any old cowhand out for an early-morning constitutional, searching for strayed dogies maybe.

Then he suddenly remembered that his father had liked riding in the early morning like this, he remembered the times he himself had rode with that silent, kindly man. It all came back then, all the horror and the hate, and he was turning back towards Billstown when he heard hoofbeats in the distance.

They seemed to be coming in the opposite direction from the town. He was curious. He reined in his horse, looked back.

He saw the rider then, coming fast, a slight figure on a rangy little cow-pony. Something familiar-looking about them both. Then as they came nearer the remote possibility became a dead certainty, and he could not check the surprised, almost shocked exclamation that rose to his lips.

Her hair streamed in the wind, her face flushed, when she reined in before him.

'I didn't expect to meet you out here, Miriam,' was all he could think to say.

She was a little breathless, but her words were clipped and sure. 'Although I was looking for you, I didn't expect to find you out here either. I was prepared to ride right into Billstown if need be.'

'Are you plumb crazy?' The exclamation was forced from him; he was still staring at her as if she was some kind of spook.

'Maybe you are the one who is crazy. They told me you'd light at Billstown and I wouldn't believe them.

34

But it looks like they were right, after all, doesn't it?'

Her tone nettled him. 'If you mean your father was right, isn't he always right?' he sneered.

'Many others beside my father were right,' she said quietly.

He matched her change of mood now. 'What do you want with me?'

'Are you leaving Billstown?'

He would not lie to her. He had never lied to her. 'To tell you the truth I was just going back there. Why?'

She seemed to take a deep breath. 'Jim Caldicott's herd was stampeded by raiders last night. Three men were killed, one of them your old boyhood friend – our old friend – Jim Blake—'

A giant hand grabbed Bert's heart, squeezed it. He hoped the pain did not show in his face. She went on remorselessly:

'The other men got away and gave the alarm. One of them said he saw you among the raiders, saw your face clearly in a flash of lightning—' She paused, staring at him, horror growing in her eyes. She knew him so well, they had been children together, with that awareness of each other that children have. She had that awareness now – it would have been useless to lie to her.

'You were with them,' she burst out. 'You were! I can see it in your face.'

Her tone lashed him and at first he seemed to flinch. Then it was as if he realized who he was, what he was; a gust of rage seized him. 'What if I was with them?' he retorted savagely. 'I swore to fight the

35

people who shamed my father and killed him. Could I fight them alone?'

It was her turn to flinch. 'But Jim Blake. Jim who–'

'I didn't know Jim was there. I didn't think Jim would ever work for people like the Caldicotts. Anyway, I didn't do any shooting, I swear that. It wasn't me who killed Jim–'

The girl broke in again – though it was almost as if she was talking to herself. 'You're lost – lost! There is nothing I can do for you any more.'

'You better get back where you came from, Miriam,' he said roughly. 'It isn't safe out here.'

She lowered her head, turned her horse about. Without another word she rode off. He wanted to call her back, tell her that it was not right for them to part this way, but he did not do so. He saw that she was quirting her horse to a breakneck speed, she who loved horses so much.

As he turned away, horse and rider were just a dust-puff in the distance. It was almost as if she had never been here.

What had been her motive in coming? Women were funny creatures!

That one had as much spunk as the average man. He wondered uneasily whether he himself was really such a tough hombre as he pretended to be.

Ahead of him a rider came from the jumble of rocks and streaked for town. It was too far away for Bert to recognize him. Looked like the skunk had been in hiding, watching. Bert hesitated no longer, but set off in pursuit.

The other man had too big a start. He disappeared

into town. Bert dismounted outside Con Bryer's place and looked the cayuses over at the hitch-rack there. None of them looked like they had recently been ridden hard. The street was empty of humans except for an old-timer resting against a stoop a few yards away. Bert went across to him, only to discover he was fast asleep. Looked like it would've taken a stampede of longhorns to wake him. Bert gave up his quest as a bad job and entered the saloon.

CHAPTER 4

It was still early, the place empty except for Bucky, who was mopping the floor. He looked up, but didn't seem so surprised at seeing Bert as he might have been.

'Up early, Kid, ain't you?'

'I've been for a constitutional. Habit of a lifetime – such as my lifetime is.'

'Wal, you'll have to keep earlier hours than you did last night, younker, or you won't be able to keep up that habit. Unless you want to make an early permanent visit to Boothill, that is.'

'I figure there are plenty other ways to get an early trip up the hill.'

'There are that,' said Bucky, shrewdly. Then he asked: 'Are you sorry you went with the boys last night, Kid?'

'Nope,' said Bert, and right then he meant it.

'Anybody else been in this mornin'?' he asked casually.

Bucky raised his eyebrows. 'Are you joshing? After the shindig last night d'yuh think the boys 'ud be up early. They're probably lyin' with their heads under the clothes.' He grinned. 'You'll larn.'

'How about you? You're up early enough.'

'I'm used to it. Besides I don't go riding anymore o' nights an' get myself all tuckered out.'

'You used to ride with the boys, Bucky!' It was half a question, half a statement.

The big man gave an indefinite grunt. Bert had noticed that he often used grunts instead of conversation. And the grunts never meant anything. A deep one was Bucky. Bert knew it was against the code of the West to ask questions, particularly in a community like Billstown. But perversity would have made him go on, had not a slight diversion occurred.

There were footsteps on the stairs and then Jack Tremaine came into view. His sparse colourless hair stood on end and he was rubbing his eyes.

'Mornin'.'

'Mornin',' the two men answered him.

'Beat me to it, huh, Kid?' he went on.

'Yeah, I've always been used to getting up early.'

There he went again, explaining himself. He had become very guarded and suspicious since he hit Billstown. And he was still thinking of the rider who had streaked away from him on the range hardly a few minutes ago.

Jack had no further comment to make, but turned to Bucky and asked: 'Gonna rustle up some chow, old-timer?'

'Sure.' The big man waddled off to the kitchen.

'Let's light, Kid.' Jack led the way to the small dining-room used exclusively by the boys. And there, one by one, they put in an appearance.

Bert watched them closely, wondering if it was one of them who had been spying on Miriam and him out on the range. There was no way of telling, of course. They were a sullen lot in the early morning. A late night, its exploits turned to dust and ashes in their mouths, they hadn't stayed with their heads under the clothes the way Bucky had figured. Bert wondered whether there was some particular reason for them all rising so early. Bert found himself staring at the scowling Candy, and lowered his eyes. He didn't want to precipitate another quarrel yet awhile.

Soon they were all there. Laredo Tim Baggs, Lenny the horse-thief and wrangler, Grado, Bear the half-breed, Bruiser Pink, huge, blinking – all of them except Med Jones and the boss.

Then Con Bryer entered, said 'Good morning' quietly and seated himself. Bucky was not long behind him with the chow. Then to Bert's astonishment, Con Bryer, immaculate as ever, and twice as deadly, mumbled grace.

They were eating when Con, looking around him, said: 'Wait a minute.' Everybody downed their trencherman tools. This man's word was law.

'Where's Med?'

'Drunk in bed as usual,' said Lenny, with malicious amusement.

Con's voice was soft then, his eyes hooded. 'I said everybody was to be here. Go get him, Jack.'

'The ol' buzzard don't mean any harm, Con.'

'Go get him!'

41

Jack shrugged and went. Nobody started to eat again.

Presently there were footsteps on the stairs again, heavy, uncertain ones now besides the catlike ones, hardly audible, of Jack Tremaine. Nobody moved or said a word. Bert discovered that all his muscles and nerves were tensed as if he waited for something terrible to happen. Med came in first, hesitantly. He did not look at anybody as he sat down.

Con Bryer shouted: 'Bring Med a nice big helping, Bucky!'

'You bet!'

One of the men chuckled. Jack Tremaine reseated himself. The notorious gunfighter watched his half-brother, Con, very closely.

Bucky came in with a huge, steaming plate of food and placed it before Med Jones. The old man looked at it then lowered his head. His gnarled fingers played with his knife and fork but did not raise them to the plate.

'What're you waiting for, Med?' said Con. 'Bucky's done you proud.'

Bruiser Pink giggled inanely.

'I couldn't eat a thing, Con,' mumbled the old man.

'You'll eat it,' said Con in the deadly quiet, 'or I'll get two of the boys to ram it down your throat.'

The old man looked up. There was a little fire in his eyes. 'You wouldn't do that, Con?'

'Wouldn't I? Just try me.'

'But I couldn't eat it, Con. I – I'd embarrass everybody.' The old man's bowed shoulders straightened

42

a little. He pushed the heaped plate away from him.

'Bruiser – Grado,' ordered the boss, 'feed it to him.'

Bruiser giggled again as he rose. Grado's dark face was as impassive as ever. Only the gleam in his eyes betokened his sadistic anticipation. The two men advanced on the old doctor, one on each side, so that he couldn't get past them. He looked from one to the other of them as he slowly pushed his chair back. There was no sign of drunkenness or tiredness about him now. He just looked a little bewildered, a little scared. 'You can't do it, Con,' he said. But he didn't seem to be talking to anybody in particular anymore.

'Eat your nice breakfast, Med,' crooned Bruiser Pink, and giggled some more.

Grado Bear said nothing.

Med pushed his chair a little further back so that he could watch both men as they came nearer. Suddenly, his dignity came back, and with it a derringer quickly into his gnarled fist. 'I'll kill the first man who touches me,' he said.

Grado and Bruiser stopped moving, as if they had become petrified. Their slow wits didn't take in things right off; they gawped at the doc as if he had suddenly grown two heads; they understood the menace of the wicked little gun far more than they would ever understand the old man. That gun was the only thing that would have stopped them.

For a moment there was dead silence, then Jack Tremaine said: 'You can push a man just so far.' He was looking at his half-brother, and it seemed to the watching Bert Cave that there was a challenge in that look.

Con met the glance and threw it back. 'I guess you're right, Jack,' he said. He turned his head. 'Get back to your seats, you two hulks, before Med perforates one of you.'

They did as they were told. Med put his gun away. Con went on: 'You'll try an' eat a mite of breakfast for me now, won't you, old-timer?'

Med smiled gravely. Finally he said: 'I feel better already. Maybe I'll be calling for another plateful.' Somebody laughed. Everybody started to eat. The drama was over.

Bert figured maybe this was just Con's ultra-clever way of amusing himself. It seemed to the younker, however, that the final word had been given, quietly, by the deadly Jack. Bert didn't despise Med Jones now.

This short passage had taught the younker something that it might have taken him years to learn: that a man's spirit is never really conquered, will rise suddenly from the dust. He wondered anew at the men around him, these strange bed-fellows. The suave, clever gambler from the coast; the famous killer with the cold eyes and gentle smile; the punch-drunk bare-knuckle fighter; the ignorant, primeval half-Indian; the scarfaced outlaw, Baggs of Laredo; the snakelike treacherous Lenny with his love of good horseflesh, strange in such a man; the young hellion, Candy. These were the inner ring of the gang. And now he was one of them.

And suddenly Bert realized that Con was looking

right at him, almost as if reading his thoughts. 'And how do you feel this morning, Kid?'

'Fine, thanks.' Bert wondered if Con had put the whole show on just for his benefit. Then he cursed himself for being bigheaded. Why would Con Bryer want to impress him? Anyway, the boss couldn't have known how the old doctor would react. Or could he?

'Life has some strange surprises, doesn't it?' Con remarked cryptically, and attacked his meal again.

Not until he had cleaned his plate and had his fill of thick, hot coffee did he speak again. And then it was to tell them of his reason for calling this early meeting. Today, whether they had expected it or not, was going to be a busy one. They were not going to be allowed to curl up and lick their wounds. He gave out with the orders.

Candy and Grado were to go to Faro Creek and keep their eyes and ears open. Neither of them were known there, so they would be all right as long as they kept out of trouble. Bruiser and Baggs were to patrol the range in the same territory, for the same purpose. They would have to be even less obtrusive than Candy and his pard, for the Faro Creek ranch-hands would be sure to be keeping their eyes open for suspicious strangers.

'Don't get yourselves lynched,' said Con with grim humour.

'Trust us, boss,' said the man from Laredo laconically.

One of Con's many minions had got kicked in the belly in a fight and was in a bad way. Med Jones had to go see what he could do for the poor devil.

Of the 'inner ring' that left only Jack Tremaine and Bert Cave. Con said he didn't want the Kid to show his face anywhere near Faro Creek. So Bert had to stick around Billstown, get to know the place.

'I got to go out of town myself on business,' went on the boss. 'If anything crops up in my absence, you report to Jack as usual. Jack – you better stay here with the Kid.'

The gunfighter exchanged glances with Bert and smiled thinly. 'Sure, Con.'

'Get goin', all of you,' said the boss. They filed out. That afternoon, after a good meal, Bert joined Jack out back in the latter's usual spare-time diversion, target practice. A row of cans on a picket fence, a hand fanning the hammer of a gun, the cans tumbling, each one drilled dead centre. A coin tossed into the air, a draw that was a thing of wonder, gun-chambers emptied, the coin kept spinning in the air until it finally fell, a mere speck of chewed-up metal.

Bert had never before seen shooting like it.

'You try,' said Jack.

Bert managed to hit the cans, but none of them dead centre. He missed the tossed coin entirely. 'Looks like I'll have to take you in hand,' said Jack.

'I'll take you up on that,' Bert told him, greatly daring.

But Jack only smiled his gentle smile and said: 'All right. Here, try it again.' He tossed the coin. This time Bert managed to chip it before it fell. 'Your draw isn't nearly fast enough,' said Jack. 'That's the first item on the agenda.'

46

The echoes died. From behind the two men came a silvery ripple of laughter.

Bert Cave turned and saw the girl.

Her golden hair was so elaborately curled that it did not look quite real. Her eyes were big, her face pert and pretty. She wore some kind of a vivid robe, all red. It was called a house-coat but Bert did not know that. It moulded her figure like a second skin. She had a full, high figure, a slim waist with a slight sensuous bulge of midriff, flowing hips. Bert had never seen a woman dressed like that and still appearing to be almost naked. It made him feel uncomfortable.

'You shouldn't be out here like that, Estelle,' said Jack Tremaine.

She dimpled, gave Bert a sidelong, inviting glance. 'I just wanted to take a look at the new boy. He's kinda handsome, isn't he?' Her voice was husky, sexy, like the rest of her.

'Go back in,' said Jack, and there was iron in his voice now.

She shrugged and went.

'Who's that?' asked Bert.

'That's Con's girl, Estelle May. She came here to sing in the saloon, and Con adopted her. She's sticking longer than the others. Keep away from her, Kid. She likes to think she has a lot of influence with Con. She's a troublemaker.'

'She's kinda young.'

'To be a dance-hall girl or to be Con's mistress?'

Jack asked the questions and answered them himself, though cryptically. 'Even young sidewinders

47

can bite,' he said. He tossed a coin, shot it coolly and
savagely to pieces.

CHAPTER 5

The day passed. The boys all returned unscathed. Then, finally, Con put in an appearance once more, after whatever mysterious journey that had taken up his time. They all met in the eating-parlour again, and over a hot meal gave their reports and compared notes.

Candy said there wasn't much going on at Faro Creek. Not much that would worry the boss, anyway. People were talking about the raid on the Caldicott spread and boasting how they'd string up the rustlers higher than kites if they caught 'em.

'Just talk,' said Candy contemptuously. 'Nobody paid any attention to me an' Grado. We acted dumb-an' listened. Seems that the Caldicott stock stampeded to hell an' gone, an' they're still searching for most of it. Caldicott's hired extra men to help in the rounding up. We also heard that he's gonna import gunslingers from the Pecos, in case the – er – rustlers try any more tricks.' Candy chuckled. 'That may be only rumour, o' course.'

He broke off, still grinning inanely. Finally, Con

49

said impatiently: 'All right, what's so funny?'

'The Mayor held a meeting in front of that place he calls his 'chambers'. He made a speech full of how sorry he was for the rancher who had been our victim and the young cowhands who had been so foully murdered.'

Candy was highly diverted by his own interpretation of the Mayor's speech. He began to chuckle again. Listening, watching from under lowered brows, Bert Cave thought he had never, from the very start, hated Candy so much as he hated him now. He noted how negligently Candy held his wounded arm in its sling. It obviously was not very bad now. The sooner it was completely all right, the better. Bert Cave badly wanted to beat Candy's head in. He hoped the sadistic young gunman would not forget to give him this opportunity.

'That ain't all,' said Candy, spluttering.

Con Bryer let his hand fall with a slap on the table-top. 'Quit foolin,' he snapped. 'If you've anything else to say, let's hear it. If not, shut up an' give somebody else a chance.'

'Sorry, boss.' Candy wiped his eyes with the back of his hand. 'In the long run the Mayor's speech was nothin' to do with rustling at all. The old goat was putting forth a resolution or somep'n. He wants the name of Faro Creek changed to somep'n else, somep'n more dignified!'

Con smiled now. 'What f'instance?'

'Craddockville, maybe,' said Bert Cave.

Everybody looked at him. 'What was that, Kid?' asked Con.

50

'Craddockville! Craddock is the Mayor's name.'

Con grinned. 'Why, sure it is. Sure, I remember now.'

Everybody was grinning now, seeing the funny side of the situation. This was particularly the case with those of them who knew the Mayor of Faro Creek by sight. And none knew him better than Bert Cave. Craddock was paunchy and pompous and small-minded and sly. He had an exaggerated sense of his own importance and, with his sly finagling behind the scenes, could do far more damage than a really dangerous man. He was a figurehead for the big boys of Faro Creek. Bert realized suddenly that Craddock was one of those he had every reason to hate. The thought sobered him.

It would be an ironical thing if Faro Creek did get to be called Craddockville. Stranger things had happened. It was Bert's experience, young though he was, that the good got the bullet in the back and the bad got the glory and the gravy.

The laughter had died down. Laredo Tim Baggs was rising to give his report.

Bruiser and he had patrolled the Caldicott and Faro Creek territory. They had been very careful, but even so had been spotted by a sizeable bunch of riders and chased a couple of miles.

'We didn't see much cattle,' said Baggs, adding, with laconic humour, 'but the humans thereabouts are as jittery as a bunch of old women with the seven-day itch.'

'Did anybody get a good look at you?' asked Con.

'Nope, not a chance. On the trail between here

and Faro Creek though, we saw four riders we've never seen in these parts before. One of them looked kinda familiar to me from the old days. If I don't miss my guess, all four of 'em are professional troubleshooters.'

'So the rumour Candy and Grado heard might be the truth, after all?'

'Could be. Those boys could've been heading for Faro or the Caldicott Ranch.'

'They haven't wasted much time,' said Con. 'Still, they won't faze us none. We'll take care of those troubleshooters or whatever they are when the need arises.'

There were murmurs of assent from all round the table. Then Con went on: 'We're gonna let the Faro territory stew for a while, anyway. I've got my eye on another little fat plum for us.' He paused. Then added reflectively:

'I haven't knocked over a bank since I was in knee-britches.'

'There ain't a bank anywhere near here, boss,' put in Grado Bear.

Con glared at him. It was obvious to everybody that the dumb half-breed had spoken out of turn.

'Do we have to keep on fouling our own backyard,' snarled the boss.

'No, boss, but I – uh—' The mahogany-faced man trailed off into incoherent mumbles.

Con enjoyed his minion's discomfiture, and when he spoke again he was the soul of affability once more.

'We're gonna travel. By train if need be. Today,

while you suckers were playing hide an' seek with your own apron-strings, I was setting up a sweet little job for you almost a hundred miles from here. Did any of yuh ever hear of Aceville?'

'I did hear talk of it,' said Baggs. 'It's one o' them new trail-towns, ain't it? What they call a boom-town.'

'Boom-town is right,' said Con. 'It's a cattle-buying centre. People drive their stock to the markets there from all over the place, so that buyers from the big Eastern combines can look it over. The place is bursting with dinero an' they've only got one bank. It's well guarded, but you could open the so-called strong-room with a can opener. We can take care of the guards. The rest'll be easy. The day after tomorrow there's a big cattleman's convention or suchlike taking place there. I have reason to believe the bank will be fuller than ever of dinero, positively cracking at the seams. At the same time the revellers will be full of hooch and we mightn't get much opposition.'

'We'll take care o' that,' said Lenny the wrangler. 'I gotta hand it to you, Con.'

The boss took no notice of this sycophantic outburst; went on: 'We'll start tomorrow morning. I'll go into things more definitely when we get to the other end. I don't want any forgetfulness or mistakes. We want a big haul and we want to all come back in one piece. We won't leave any wounded singers behind, believe me.' His hard, sardonic glance swept the faces around the table. His meaning was plain.

He rose. 'Will you come up to the office with me, Jack?'

His *segunda* followed him out. The meeting was over.

Med Jones rose, came around the table to Candy. 'Let me have a look at that wound of yours, son.'

'It's all right,' said Candy. 'I had it out o' the sling at Faro Creek so I wouldn't draw attention to myself.' His glance flickered across the table towards Bert Cave.

The two young men grinned at each other wolfishly.

From outside came the sounds of revelry. Pretty soon all the boys joined the crowd in the bar-room.

Bert Cave joined Baggs, Grado and Med in a game of poker. Time passed. Looking up during a lull in the game, the Kid saw Estelle May at the head of the stairs. She seemed to be looking at him, it was almost as if she signalled to him. She quickly disappeared. Bert, who was winning himself quite a stack, got on with the game, but the vision of Estelle kept obtruding. He had only seen her twice, but knew her for an irritating witch. He began to lose again.

He finished up by losing quite a pile. He was glad to get in bed that night.

But still he could not sleep.

Quite suddenly he had women on the brain. It was something that had never happened to him before. Until the other day he had barely realized that his old playmate Miriam was grown up to be a beautiful and desirable young woman. Now the sight of her as she was on the last time they met haunted his half-awake dreams. The last words she had spoken to him echoed over and over in his mind:

'There is nothing I can do for you anymore. You're lost – lost.

'Lost— Lost—'

It came with the range-wind outside, the wind they had often shared together. It rose to a whining, maddening refrain and suddenly he couldn't stand it anymore. Women! Judging by what he'd seen and heard of them, they were always whining about something. A man was a fool to get himself tangled up with them. That's what all the boys said when they swapped their lewd tales; none of the boys took women seriously.

He cursed softly under his breath, as if Miriam was there and he was cursing her for her interference. Then he realized what a childish fool he was and he tried to sleep, or at least to think of something else.

And now Estelle obtruded herself. Con's woman; he shouldn't be bothering his head about Con's woman!

But before he slept it was almost as if she was in the room with him and he didn't know what to think about that.

He awakened to the sound of shots. Poking his head out of the window he spotted Jack at his target practice. The gunman, who seemed to have senses like a cat, whirled and saw him.

'Hallo, Kid. It's time you quit pounding your ear. C'mon down, I've got another trick to show you.'

The trick consisted of spinning a gun by its triggerguard and, as it smacked into the palm of the hand after the third revolution, thumbing the hammer, fetching cans off the fence like they had been whisked away by an invisible hand.

Like most gunfighters, Jack never pulled trigger. He always thumbed the hammer. He had the triggers of his guns filed off so they would not get in his way. Thumbing the hammer, or 'fanning it' with the free hand was a quicker method of pumping lead than any other the makers of hand-guns had yet been able to devise.

Bert attempted this new trick of Jack's, but most of his shots went wild.

'You better quit 'fore you shoot your foot off,' said the gunman with grim humour. 'You're too stiff an' jerky; you gotta loosen up, let your muscles relax. Let's see your draw again.'

Bert made it, fetched a can neatly off the fence with a snap shot. Jack nodded approvingly. 'That's better.'

Bert sheathed his gun again. Jack took hold of his hand, turned it palm upwards. 'You've got the paws of a gunfighter, anyway,' he grinned mirthlessly. 'They're kinda calloused though – hard work, I guess. That will never do. You've got to take care of your hands. You've got to treat them gently, you might hold your life in them at any time.'

The gunfighter was revolving his own hands now for the young man's inspection. Without touching them, Bert inspected them.

A gunfighter's smooth, brown prehensile, murderous hands.

'You see,' said Jack softly.

Bert did not need to answer, but he did so.

'I see,' he echoed.

56

Bucky yelled 'Come an' git it!' It was breakfast time. And then the boys were assembling for the big trip, and the 'plum of a job' at the end of it.

CHAPTER 6

To avoid any possibility of being identified in Aceville, the Bryer boys came in in two sections on two different trains, and even then kept strictly apart, no more than a pair at a time. They took lodgings in different parts of the town. Con had gotten everything organised beforehand.

Bert Cave once again paired up with Jack Tremaine. Maybe Con wanted his right-hand man to keep an eye on the new recruit. Though there may have been another reason. The notorious gunfighter had left his mark in many parts of the lawless south west, and it was inevitable that he would be recognized in Aceville. A few people greeted him, in fact, though, for the most part, warily. Could be, however, that this young companion (to some people he looked a little too young to be dangerous) was the perfect foil for Jack's quiet deadliness. Jack was too old and salty a hand to go deliberately looking for trouble (unless he was paid to do so); but he was, by virtue of his profession and notoriety, a man calculated to invite trouble if only in the person of half-drunken waddies who wanted to test his speed, wanted to make a name for themselves. Though the only name they were likely to make for themselves (some did!) was that of having been untimely cut down by the West's fastest gun.

Bert, 'the Kid', could not help being a little proud of being seen with Jack Tremaine. Some day people would gaze after him this way – gaze at him alone – touch their hats, call him 'Mister'. He had been downtrodden enough. He would be top-dog. People would have cause to remember his name too. Some would die remembering it, remembering the raw deal they had once given an older man of the same name, a man who had been too straight, too inoffensive.

Jack and Bert got a room at a two-storeyed frame establishment, which, compared to most of the joints, was a cowboy's dream of home.

The boys were given a day in which to familiarise themselves with the layout of the town, and in particular the area around the bank. They passed each other – two by two – on the streets, and gave no sign of recognition. It was all part of the plan. They played their parts well, of cowhands on a spree, but were careful not to drink too much or get tangled up with women or trouble. So far as most of them were concerned, women and trouble usually came pretty close together. They were owlhooters to the core, had gotten their experience in a hard and vicious school: they knew that the time for liquor and women was after the job had been tied up and put behind them. It meant sudden death at the hands of his comrades for the man who did anything to jeopardise their chances at a time like this.

That night, the eve of the job, the men rode away from town at intervals, in pairs, and made their way by devious routes to the place of rendezvous. This was easy to find, for after instructions from Jack, they had taken note of it from the train windows on their ways into Aceville. It was a huge rock outcrop rising from the plain, known locally, because of its shape, as the Cockeyed Sombrero. At its base and by the light of a tiny fire, Con drew diagrams in the sand with a pointed stick and gave them all their final instructions.

The following day was the first day of the rodeo which always took place during the Cattlemen's Convention. This night, while the gang crouched at the misshapen base of the Cockeyed Sombrero, Aceville was busting its seams with jollification. Tomorrow morning everybody who didn't have to be at business would sleep late, the town would be quiet. This was just the time, Con opined, when the guards at the bank would be keeping their eyes peeled for trouble. However, in the early afternoon the rodeo really got under way with the bronco-busting, bull-dozing and roping contests. Everybody who could be there would be. At three o'clock one of the West's champion horsemen, Pete Jarado, was riding an unbeaten 'killer' called Dynamite. Maybe, after such a nice quiet morning, one or two of the bank guards would slip away to watch this epoch-making performance.

At least, the guards' vigilance would have relaxed.

So, concluded Con, quarter past three was the time that, so far as the Bryer gang was concerned anway, the balloon went up.

Crouched over the flickering fire, glancing at the hard, crafty faces around him, Bert Cave learned that for the purpose of the raid he would part company with Jack Tremaine and help Med Jones to hold the horses ready. Bert knew it was useless to argue against this decision. He wasn't sure that he wanted to argue, anyway. He was letting things take their course. His time would come. He was the youngest member of the band, except maybe for Candy, and by far the least experienced. It was right he should be relegated to a menial task.

The horses were to be split into two separate bunches, with four 'reserves' in case any of them got hit by flying lead. Con had left very little to chance. The boys had brought their own mounts along in the van of the train, as most visitors had done. Con had gotten the extra four from an unknown source in town.

Bert Cave learned from Con's diagram in the sand that he would be in charge of the first batch of horses and, from his position, would be able to see what was going on at the bank. He might even have to take a hand if things got sticky.

'Yuh might get a chance to show off your new-found shootin' ability, Kid,' said Jack Tremaine laconically.

Med Jones, though he always rode with the gang, never did any shooting. He always said it was his job to heal, not hurt.

'Goshdarned ol' hypocrite,' said Candy.

'Naw, it's just his excuse,' said another man. 'He couldn't hit a barn door if he had his foot agin it.'

There was much laughing and back-slapping until Con said: 'Quiet, you damned fools, there might be others riding out here tonight, besides ourselves.'

There was silence then, except for the soughing of the nightwinds. Then the boss gave out with his final instructions. 'Make sure all your guns are in perfect trim, holsters well greased, and you have plenty of cartridges. Tim Baggs, you take charge of the dynamite, I'm depending on you.'

'I've never let you down yet,' said the man from Laredo.

'All right. Let's move. Jack – Kid – you go first.'

For those two it was a silent ride back to town. Once Bert ventured on conversation, but only received monosyllables in return.

When they hit Main Street, however, Jack broke his silence. 'I'm gonna turn in, Kid. I ain't as young as I useter be. I guess you want to kick your heels a while longer, so I'll bid you goodnight.'

Bert hadn't thought about what he aimed to do, but it seemed to him that Jack suddenly wanted to get rid of him. So he wished the older man 'goodnight' and steered his horse towards one of the saloons. He was glad to learn that Jack didn't figure that the new recruit needed watching all the time.

The flimsy, false-fronted clapboard joint called 'The Five in Hand' was cracking at the seams. The smoke made a man's eyes smart, his vision difficult until he got used to the atmosphere. The noise was indescribable. Bert wriggled his lean form to the bar and had a couple of drinks. Then he went over to watch the games. A perspiring fat man in a multi-coloured fancy waistcoat was taking bets on tomorrow's rodeo contests. At a faro table near to him Bert spotted Candy Sampson and Grado Bear.

At the same time they saw him, and the leering Candy called: 'Where's your wet nurse, Kid?'

Bert bit off the retort that had risen to his lips, watched Grado grab Candy's arm, speak urgently into his ear. No doubt the half-breed was reminding his reckless companion of Con's no-talk rule. The younker scowled, bent his head to the game once more. Bert quickly passed on. There was no sign of anything being wrong with Candy's arm now. Pretty soon he'd be able to beat that poisonous character's ears down.

Bert was more accustomed to the open air than the sawdust and the smoke. His head began to spin. He made his way from the joint.

A large tent was pitched on the waste-lot nearby. A red lamp hung from its ridge-pole. A fat, painted woman bragged, in a voice that could have reached to the Gulf, of the purity and beauty of her 'gels'.

Bert spat dryly, plodded on, leading his horse. The night air was cool to his face and was full of the nostalgic odours of sage and juniper. He remembered the times his dad and he had ridden together on such nights as this one, and a lump rose to his throat.

But now was not the time for weakness of any kind. Cursing himself, he hitched his horse to another tie-rail, entered another 'sporting-house'. This was a smaller place than the last, a Mexican-style cantina-cum-saloon. He was not likely to meet any of his new 'friends' in here.

For a change he took a glass of tequila. A dark-faced man played a guitar in a corner and hummed a Spanish lament, there was the click of dice and the murmur of a croupier intoning the odds. Bert took a couple more drinks and finally got drowsy and wended his way homewards.

Jack Tremaine was snoring gently in the other truckle bed. There was a chair placed in a strategic position between Jack's bed and the door. Jack's gunbelt hung over the bedrail, but its holster was empty. Bert knew that the gunfighter always slept with his Colt beneath his pillow within easy reach of his hand.

The snoring ceased and Jack spoke and Bert realized his friend had been playing possum after all – until he had ascertained who it was who had entered. Eternal vigilance must be the watchword of him and his kind.

'How did things go, Kid?'

'All right.'

'No trouble?'

'No trouble.'

'Goodnight.'

'Goodnight.'

The bed creaked. Jack breathed gently, regularly.

Bert lay down. Finally he reached for his own gun and placed it under his pillow.

He was learning fast.

He slept.

*

The street was bathed in sunshine so brilliant that Bert had to squint his eyes against it. A couple of times he looked back to receive an encouraging wave from Med. The old man had gotten some booze from some place and was airily confident that everything would go well.

The street was deserted. The boys, in ones and twos, were moving in, elongated shapes spearing from the shadows into the sunshine. Jack Tremaine came into view, walking in the roadway. His limp seemed more pronounced than ever. Finally, when he was almost abreast of the bank he halted and sank into a sitting position on the edge of the boardwalk. He took off his riding-boot, turned it upside down, shook it reflectively. He let it fall while he rolled himself a smoke and lit it.

He was putting the boot back on again when Con Bryer came briskly along the boardwalk, the clack-clack of his boots awakening the echoes. He was, as usual, stylishly dressed. A leather brief-case was tucked under his arm. He looked every inch a Western businessman, or maybe a buyer for a big Eastern concern.

He did not even glance in Jack's direction. He turned briskly into the bank.

Jack rose slowly to his feet. The watching Kid knew that the gunfighter must be counting the seconds. Jack, however, looked like he hadn't a care in the world. He stamped his boot experimentally. From the direction of the rodeo ground came a subdued roaring.

Jack stepped on to the boardwalk. Despite his gammy leg he moved with incredible swiftness and his footsteps awakened no echoes.

As he moved into the bank, the other men came out of their partial concealment, moving across the baked cart-rutted sod and along the boardwalk. Candy Sampson, on his toes, almost running. Grado Bear, his brown face set as if carved from granite. Lean, scarfaced Tim Baggs, a brown-paper bundle under his arm, moving more swiftly than any of them.

And the rest of them. No attempt at silence now. Feet scurrying and clattering. Tim Baggs was first through the door. From inside the bank came the report of a single shot.

The watching Kid started. He knew that Con had stipulated no shooting if it could possibly be helped. Not that Con was a particularly humane man. He objected to the noise. The heavy end of a gun could be just as effective and far more silent if anybody cut up rough. Time enough for a big bang when, in the last stage of the job, the dynamite went off. Maybe the dynamite wouldn't be needed, anyway.

Bert wondered who had fired the shot. Con – Jack – or one of the other side? There hadn't been time for Tim Baggs to do any shooting. Grado Bear had gone in there too now. So had Candy Sampson. The doors had stopped swinging. Bruiser Pink and Lenny the wrangler stood outside then, their hands on their guns. Other men kept watch at vantage points. From the direction of the rodeo ground came another burst of cheering. Dust settled in the sunbeams.

The sun struck the back of Bert Cave's neck with a steady, insistent heat. He turned and gave Med the signal. The old man acknowledged it. Bert edged his horses forward a little, so that the men would be able to see them as soon as they left the bank. He looked back to see if Med was doing the same. It was then that he saw the man.

He came negligently around the corner. He was youngish, looked like a cowhand. His thumbs were hooked into his belt. His battered Stetson was tilted over his eyes and a cigarette angled from the corner of his mouth.

He didn't seem to notice Med, passed him, came on towards Bert. The latter steeled himself. He knew he would have to slug this character before he got in sight of the bank and saw Bruiser and Lenny in their suggestive poses.

The man turned before reaching Bert and meandered off down a side street. Evidently he hadn't heard the shot. Bert exchanged a congratulatory glance with Med, breathed a sigh of relief. He hoped, however, that the leisurely character got well out of earshot before anything else went off.

Hardly was the thought dissipated into the air than there was another shot from inside the bank.

Things happened so quickly after this that Bert didn't have any more time to think about the nonchalant character.

Somebody shouted. Bruiser Pink moved into the bank. Lenny the wrangler, squinting in the sunlight, exchanged a scowling glance with Bert. The latter passed the signal on to Med, who began to bring his horses forward preparatory to joining them up with Bert's bunch.

Things hadn't gone as planned. The Kid had to take a hand. He crossed the street swiftly. Lenny darted into the bank. Bert took his place on the boardwalk. He had butterflies in his stomach. There was a terrible blatter of shots from inside the bank. Instantly Bert was cool, savage. He dropped his hand to his gun, peered about him.

He heard the doors thud back, and whirled, drawing his gun.

Bruiser Pink staggered out. Both his hands were pressed to his belly and there was a terrible, puzzled look on his battered bovine face. Blood welled sluggishly through his interlaced fingers. He looked right through Bert, not seeing him. There was death in his little eyes. He staggered to the edge of the boardwalk and pitched from it, to lie still, spreadeagled.

The doors swung slowly. Blue smoke drifted through them. From behind them came the terrible high sobbing of a man in agony. There was a single shot and the sound stopped. There was silence then, and looking about him in the sunshine, Bert Cave felt himself trembling. The street was empty. The shadows stood on the corners. Med waited with the horses.

The explosion from the bank seemed to split the silence apart. Bert was rocked on his heels by the suddenness of it.

The echoes died away and the silence pulsated like a living brain. Then the men began to come out. They came out backward, each one with a gunny-sack in one hand and a gun in the other. Con and Jack came last, the latter covering his half-brother's retreat – for Con had a gunny-sack in one hand and his brief-case, bulging now, in the other.

'Let's go,' said Con. He paused for an infinitesimal moment by Bruiser Pink. 'Grado – Tim – grab him. We don't want to leave any clues behind.'

'Some clue,' said the man from Laredo. He grinned as if he was at a tea-party as he helped Grado Bear to lift the huge carcase of the ex-pug.

Evidently there was still danger back there in the bank. The boys didn't take any chances, anyway. They were still half-turned, guns elevated, as they scuttled towards the horses.

Bert Cave saw the face at the back window, the shine of the lifted gun. But the face wasn't turned in his direction, the gun not pointed at him. Inherent fairness caused him to hesitate a fraction of a second. Shots rang out from beside him. Half-turning, he saw Candy Sampson crouching, his teeth showing in a snarl as he thumbed the hammer of his gun. The face disappeared. Candy whirled towards Bert, almost as if he meant to blast him down too, where he stood. Con yelled: 'Come on, come on!' Then they were all moving again, other men coming out of hiding to join them. All was quiet now back at the bank.

When another shot was fired it startled everybody. Those of the men who had not reached the horses tried to look in every direction at once. A lanky individual who had been keeping watch at a corner screamed shrilly, staggered forward and fell on his face. Then the attackers came into view.

Leading them was the nonchalant young cowboy who had passed between Med and the Kid not long before. He didn't look nonchalant now and there was a gun in his fist. It spoke. Another member of the Bryer gang bit the dust. The rest of them ran for the horses, mounted. It was Tim Baggs who plugged the young cowboy and, watching him fall, Bert Cave felt a strange sadness: he had seemed such a happy-go-lucky cuss – clever too.

A slug tugged at the brim of the Kid's hat. He mounted among the rest, urged his horse forward. Slugs flew among them like angry hornets. A man grunted, another yelled aloud with pain. A horse screamed shrilly and crumpled, throwing its rider. As the man was scrambling for another mount, a slug slammed into his shoulder. He was helped on to the horse by Med and lay along the saddle, panting.

'Let's get goin' before reinforcements arrive,' yelled Con shrilly.

They swept away, leaving their dead behind them, except Bruiser Pink, honoured in death far more than he had ever been in life. All the gang could hope was that those they had left behind could not talk, had indeed cashed in their chips. And, further-more, that they had not been carrying any incrimi-nating evidence around with them.

Most of the townsfolk, having been given the alarm while they were at the rodeo, hadn't stopped to get horses. Here was where they had made their mistake.

The Bryer gang got clean away. They couldn't risk

hopping a train this time, so had to ride all the way home. But their horses were hand-picked and fresh. They made it all right.

CHAPTER 7

It had been a good haul. But the job hadn't gone at all the way Con had planned. Far from it.

Four men killed. Three wounded. Two of the bankclerks had cut up rough and had to be shot. Con hadn't reckoned with this: such poorly-paid minions weren't usually so brave. Con couldn't figure, either, how the alarm had been given so quickly. Med and the Kid could have enlightened him, but wisely kept their mouths shut.

The latter came in for a lacing in any case. 'I didn't see you do any shooting, Kid,' snarled the boss. 'You're too damn slow. That galoot at the window – you could've got him before Candy did. While you were making up your mind he could've mowed a couple of us down.'

'The Kid's jinx was holdin' him again,' jeered Candy Sampson.

Bert hadn't known that his momentary hesitation had been spotted by anyone except Candy. He took the boss's reprimand with equanimity. But Candy was a different proposition. Bert wheeled on him; he had

73

been waiting for him to open his trap.

'You're always talking outa turn,' he said softly. 'Someday somebody's gonna fill your mouth with teeth.'

Candy rose, almost knocking his chair over in his haste. 'Hold it,' rapped Con.

Candy's hand was poised over the butt of his gun. The two young men glared at each other. 'Lemme take him, boss?' pleaded Candy.

'You fit now?'

'I'm fit!'

'All right. But I'll stand no gunplay. You'll meet back of the place tomorrow morning.'

Candy let his hands fall with a little slap to his sides. 'Suits me.'

Bert merely nodded. His eyes were as hard and cruel as Con's as the latter said softly: 'We'll all retire now, then, so we can be up nice an' early.'

Jack and Bert walked side by side along the passage upstairs. Jack said softly: 'There'll be no use in trying to fight Candy fair. He knows every dirty trick in the book and, believe me, he'll use 'em. I'll be rooting for you, pardner.'

'Thanks, Jack.'

Before he slept, Bert's last thoughts were of this strange man, this killer and his unwonted kindness.

But when he awoke his thoughts were all of Candy and what he meant to do with him. Sun streamed through the window. It was a beautiful morning for a fight.

Bert put on his shirt and trousers, ran his fingers through his crisp brown hair. He left the room, padded in stockinged feet along the passage towards the bathroom. At first there was no sound: none of the boys were particularly early risers and they had all imbibed plenty of celebration liquor the night before. Bert was surprised to hear the sudden patter of feet behind him.

He paused, turned his head. 'Hallo, handsome,' said Estelle May.

She wore no paint on her face. Her eyes were drowsy, her blonde hair tousled. Yet somehow this made her look younger than ever, not so hard and metallic, more vulnerable. She wore low-heeled mules with ridiculously large red pom-pons. Her dressing-gown was of scarlet silk, and it swung open carelessly so that Bert had a glimpse of more intimate silk, peach-coloured this time, beneath it. Her legs were long and bare.

His emotions were mixed. He wondered if anybody had heard her gay greeting. 'Morning, Miss Estelle,' he said softly.

'Aren't you formal?' she said huskily. There was an open invitation in her blue eyes. Bert thought of Con Bryer and began to get uncomfortable.

He moved aside to let her pass. She moved abreast of him and seemed as if she would stop close to him in the narrow passage. But with a little mocking smile she went past him, though he felt the softness of her and smelled her faint perfume. She went into the bathroom and closed the door, and he heard the lock click.

Cursing to himself without hardly knowing the reason, he went back to his little room to wait.

A little later he heard her unmistakable steps in the passage once more. Again she seemed to pause, or maybe that was just his fevered imagination: he did not know whether he wanted her to enter his room or not. Finally, however, her footsteps faded away. He heard a door close gently somewhere along the passage.

He cursed again, dropping the cigarette he had been smoking, grinding it into the boards with his stockinged foot. There was the pungent smell of singed wool. 'Take care, you cockeyed Romeo,' he told himself. 'Do you want to burn your leg off?' He lifted the foot, inspected it, pinched out a tiny smouldering ember with thumb and forefinger.

He rose again. This time he met Jack Tremaine, usually the gang's earliest riser, in the passage. 'How do you feel, Kid?' asked the gunfighter.

'Fine, thanks.' Bert forgot about Estelle. He had more important matters to think of. In his stockinged feet he padded like a healthy young beast. He did not notice the look of admiration the older man flung at him, which changed to something else, something indefinable. Maybe Jack saw in this lithe, gangling young man something of what he had been twenty years before.

Breakfast was a silent meal. All the jubilation of the returned living had taken place the night before, and now the boys were feeling the after effects. A morose-looking Con was the last to appear.

Halfway through the meal he looked up and said: 'Divvy-up tonight. I want you all here pronto at nine o'clock – and sober.'

Faces brightened a little. The boys knew that once Con had paid out the proceeds he would loosen the reins too. They would be able to set the town alight. There was something else to look forward to also. This morning. A fight! Candy and the new boy. But they waited for Con to broach this too, and over cigarettes he did so. He was quite cheerful now, could almost be said to be licking his chops.

He said he knew the two contestants were raring to go, but he figured they ought to sit awhile and smoke and let their breakfast digest before they started milling around. He said he wanted things done properly, meaning there would be no weapons of any kind. He'd be timekeeper and referee himself, but there would be no set number of rounds. The men would fight till one of them was beaten. Each man would have a second. After all this was understood, Con added that, as far as he was concerned, nothing was barred. And at this, Candy Sampson smiled thinly, an unholy light in his eyes.

Jack Tremaine elected to second the Kid. Tim Baggs said, laconically, he'd do the same for Candy. So, finally, the men left the eating-house, each second carrying a bucket of water and a towel.

A rough ring was formed by the members of the gang and a few of the townsfolk, old owlhooters themselves for the most part, who had gotten wind of what was going to happen. Most of the percentage girls put in an appearance too, looking a little raddled in the early-morning light. This was foreign to most of them, but they were willing to risk it in order to see a good mill. They had been brought up in a hard school – or had dragged themselves down into it – their business was men, their enjoyment too; they liked to see men fight, preferably over one of them. Each one automatically picked her favourite, anyway, got ready to egg him on, screech for his opponent's blood.

The two men stripped to the waist, dropped their clothes in the dust, squatted on their haunches. Con strolled to the centre of the circle, a turnip-watch in his hand. He was hugely enjoying himself.

The Kid was the taller of the two, but considerably leaner. His brown, wedge-shaped frame was hairless except for a slight chestnut fuzz at the chest. He looked hard, supple, but almost frail against his opponent's almost squat bulk. Candy had a chest like a barrel matted with black, woolly hair.

He grinned around at the spectators, particularly the girls. 'Eat him up, Candy honah,' said one little redhead in a languid Deep South voice.

'You bet, *chiquita*.'

But Bert had his champions too, though Estelle May was not among them. He could not help wondering what had happened to her. Maybe Con had forbidden her to appear, or something. She was his favourite, a cut above these other sluts.

Or was she? Bert was savage. He crouched on one knee, waiting. He wanted to cut Candy to ribbons.

Jack was behind him, the bucket of water at his feet, the towel draped over the broken-down fence behind him. 'Take it easy, Kid,' he said softly. 'You had any experience in real rough-and-tumble?' he asked.

78

'Some.'

Con raised his hand, let it fall. 'Cut loose your curlies,' he said, and stepped nimbly out of harm's way.

Both the young men came out of their corners pretty fast. Candy's feet went slap-slap, raising little puffs of dust. His firsts were held in front of him in no particular sparring manner, but as if he intended to use them as a battering ram. He looked cruelly powerful.

The Kid had no particular stance either. He was gangling, almost awkward. He looked slightly top-heavy. There was power in those shoulders, in those long, deceptively lean arms. The right one flicked out. Candy swerved and the bony fist grazed his face. Candy bored in under his opponent's guard, sent in two thrusting body blows.

The breath went out of the Kid in a little sigh, echoed by the gasps of the crowd. But the Kid was instinctively fighting back, flinging blows rapidly. A couple of them landed with dull smacks on Candy's face, and he staggered.

The Kid drew off, grabbing wind. Candy's lips were bleeding, beginning to puff. First-blood to the Kid. The two fighters began to move in again, and then the crowd gave voice, the men baying like wolves, the women screeching like banshees. The ranks were swelling.

Candy pivotted suddenly on one heel, swinging the other foot. The boot missed the Kid's jaw by a hairsbreadth; it would surely have cracked it had the blow landed. The Kid grabbed at the swinging foot and missed, but bored in, catching Candy off-balance, slamming him on the jaw, bringing an elbow around swiftly to punish his chest as he wilted.

Grunting with pain, Candy dropped swiftly on one knee, then bounced upwards again immediately. His dark, closecropped head buffetted the Kid's flat middle. The Kid went backwards as if he had been propelled from a cannon. His heels cut grooves in the soil, raising a miniature dust-cloud.

The crowd roared. The Kid fell backwards, landed on one elbow. His face a mask of blood, Candy moved in. His aim was brutally evident: he wished to avail himself of the gentle Western prerogative of giving his man the boot.

He almost succeeded – but the Kid made an incredibly swift crablike retreat, taking himself sideways, and only received a glancing kick on his shoulder. Then as Candy whirled, the Kid was upright, meeting him. They were like warming steers now, their clash half obscured by a cloud of dust.

Con gave the signal for the end of the first round, and the two boys had to be prised apart. There were a few disgruntled murmurs from the crowd. Some of the folks didn't like this unconventional way of doing things. They wanted to see a quick and bloody end.

Still, maybe Con had the right idea. He was making things last.

But how many rounds could these two younkers last at this rate?

The Kid's lean brown body bore angry weals and was bleeding in places. But his face was comparatively unmarked. But not so his opponent's, which already looked like a lump of raw beefsteak. Candy was wincing and grimacing as the grinning Tim Baggs bathed the cuts with ice-cold water.

Jack Tremaine wiped the sweat from his boy's body, whispered: 'You're doing fine, Kid. You're faster than he is. But don't let him bear yuh down – he's strong as a bull.'

Bert managed a lopsided grin. 'Yuh durn tootin',' he said.

Con gave the word again. The boys moved out of their corners more slowly this time, warily. They circled, Candy seeming more squat and powerful than ever as he crouched. He attacked first, his feet going slap-slap in the dust, his fists working like pistons. The Kid gave ground before the savage attack. The crowd roared. They howled as the Kid suddenly dug in his heels, began to give as good as he got.

The women screamed. Now and then one of them shouted for her particular favourite, the sound wailing like a savage battle-cry above all other voices.

'Candy!'

'Kid!'

'Eee! – kill 'im, Candy! . . . Tear 'im down, Kid!'

An oldster shrieked, not with jubilation, but because one of the harpies had, in her excitement, dug her painted talons into the soft flesh of his arm. The contestants were half-obscured by dust again, so that the watchers craned and peered and somebody growled: 'Water ought to've been sprinkled on the ground 'fore they started.'

'A-aah!' A form came flying out of the dust cloud.

It was Candy, spinning and tumbling like some squat, crazy bird with a broken wing. He landed on his shoulder and rolled.

Bert Cave came after him like another bird, scrawny, crazy. 'The boot, Kid,' screamed somebody. 'The boot!'

But the Kid had a better idea. Knees bent, thrusting, he launched himself on Candy. The manoeuvre went a little wrong, only one knee punished the other man's barrel chest, forcing from him a grunt of pain. Then they were tangled together, rolling and clawing, spitting and kicking like a pair of mountain cats.

The Kid rolled free, climbed to his feet, wiping blood from his nose. Con gave the signal for the end of the round. The Kid looked around him dazely, located Jack Tremaine and wobbled across to him.

Candy rose and made as if to follow the Kid. Then he gave Con a sidelong glance, changed his mind and lurched to his own corner.

It appeared that Con was timing the rounds to suit himself. Both contestants were in a pretty bad state. Although Candy hadn't seemed to be able to reach the Kid's face in the first round, he had certainly made up for lost time in the second one. One of Bert Cave's eyes was completely closed. A thread of dried blood ran from the corner of it down to the corner of the younker's face, giving; him a devilish appearance. His longish brown hair hung in ringlets on his forehead. His body gleamed with blood and sweat. As he sat there the sun beat on to the back of his neck until Jack moved behind him, began to lave his bruises with the towel.

Tim Baggs was doing the same service for Candy, who at the moment had the appearance of a partially-slaughtered young ox. But appearances are deceptive: he was still a pretty dangerous young ox.

Jack Tremaine soaked a corner of the towel in the bucket and bathed his boy's face. Bert's vision cleared a little. He grinned wolfishly across at Candy. The latter looked murderous, as indeed he was. Con gave the signal for the third round. They leapt at each other.

And that was the way it went on. The crowd bayed like wolves while the two young men slashed each other to ribbons, tried to beat each other to a pulp.

Con made the rounds shorter. Round succeeded round. It was cruel, terrible, bloody. The boys were slower, their bodies sagging. But both had guts out of the ordinary; neither of them would give in.

Bert Cave staggered to his corner once more, back to the ministrations of Jack, ministrations which didn't seem to be doing any good any more. The sun was becoming more powerful with every second. It seemed to be trying to beat him into the ground. Suddenly he hated this burning, throbbing, pitiless sun more than he hated Candy. The sun was his enemy – his and Candy's. Suddenly he didn't hate Candy any more.

Jack was ministering to him, talking to him softly. He didn't take much notice of what Jack was saying. He was rather confused. He thought he had heard Estelle May's voice – Estelle May, rooting for him. But he hadn't spotted her.

Hell, he didn't want any yellow-haired filly rooting

for him. He'd finish this fight, he'd finish it right now. He didn't hate Candy any more; but Candy was an obstacle. He had to remove that obstacle – or the fight might go on forever. The thought that he himself might be the one to be beaten never entered his head. He was out of his corner almost before Con gave the word.

He was halfway to meet Candy when, with his sudden new-found clarity, he spotted Estelle. She was hanging out of an upstairs window. She was a picture, like the golden-haired princess of the tower in a storybook. She caught his eye and made a gesture of encouragement. Then quickly her face changed; she opened her mouth to scream; everybody seemed to be screaming.

Something that felt like a loaded stick of dynamite exploded on Bert's jaw. The world spun around him, then he hit the earth with a force that seemed to break his body in a thousand pieces.

It is surprising how quickly a man's body can piece itself together again. But in this case it wasn't allowed to stay that way. Something exploded in Bert's side, he felt something crack in there, pain knifed through him. He rolled. He saw something which looked like a huge black cannonball descending on him. Desperately he reached out, grabbed.

Candy, his ankle gripped as if by steel jaws, lost his balance. He hit the ground with stunning force, raising a miniature dust-cloud.

Bert climbed shakily to his feet. His left side felt as if it had been caved in. There was a roaring in his ears. Dimly he understood this was caused by the crowd urging him to finish his man. He stumbled forward. Stupidly he watched Candy rise, slowly, wearily. He drew back his arm, let it go. He put all his remaining strength into that blow. Candy went down again and this time he stayed down.

Bert turned slowly around, began to stumble towards where he figured his corner might be. But he never made it: the roaring was mighty, it was the roaring of black, rushing water, closing over him. Almost gratefully he sank into the flood, let it close over him, bringing oblivion.

CHAPTER 8

When he awoke, soft clouds encompassed him. The face of an angel floated above him. An angel with golden hair.

'How yuh feelin', handsome?' asked Estelle May.

The illusion was dispelled. He grinned crookedly. 'Oh, fine,' he croaked. 'Jest fine!'

Two more faces came into view. He recognized Con and Med. The latter said: 'You busted a coupla ribs. I had to bind you up. You'll be all right in next to no time.'

'Have I been out long?'

'Long enough. You cracked your head when you were falling. It's hard enough, though. There'll be no permanent harm.'

Estelle giggled. Con turned his hard gaze upon her. 'Go get the Kid a drink.'

'With water,' added Med.

'All right.'

Bert closed his eyes briefly, listening to the girl's soft footsteps pattering away, the opening and closing of the door.

'Snap out of it, Kid,' said Con.

Bert was peeved. He felt like sleeping, dreaming delicious dreams. But he opened his eyes again. 'I'm all right,' he said. 'How's Candy?'

'He'll have to lay up a while too,' said Med dryly. 'We'll keep you two ring-tailed bobcats quiet for a while, I guess.'

'You did all right, Kid,' said Con with a faint smile.

Estelle returned with a tray containing whiskey, a glass, a pitcher of water. Med poured a small portion of whiskey, doused it with water.

'F'r Pete's sake,' said Bert, but he took it and drank it. He wasn't such a hard-head as he pretended to be; the liquor made him even more drowsy.

'Get some sleep, Kid,' said Med. 'When you wake up you'll be good and ready for a five-course meal.'

'You bet—' The Kid slept.

When he awoke again twilight was creeping into the room. His body felt stiff, as if it was encased in plaster, but there was a delicious numbness. When he tried to move, however, a shaft of pain punished his side.

He spotted his sack of makings and a book of lucifers on the bedside table and managed to reach them. He made himself a smoke, lit up.

He was at the end of his second cigarette and staring reflectively at the ceiling when the•door was rapped. He started: he had not heard footsteps in the passage. For a moment of time he wished his gun was at hand. But his gunbelt was hung over a chair out of reach of his hand. He realized he was already obeying the instincts of the born owlhooter. Cautiously he called 'Come in.'

Estelle May entered with a tray of steaming food. It was almost dark now. He could see her figure, slim yet voluptuous, and the pale oval of her face.

'Could you handle this, handsome?' she asked softly.

'I certainly could.'

She crossed the room and placed the tray on the table beside the bed. She struck a match and lit the hurricane lantern. He winced with pain as he levered himself towards a sitting position. She turned her head and saw his discomfort. With seeming impetuosity she put her arms around his shoulders and helped him up.

Between pants she said: 'I fixed it with Bucky – so – I could – bring your grub up.'

She smiled at him provocatively. Next moment his arms had gone round her too and he was kissing her, and if there was any pain now it didn't faze him at all.

They moved apart when there was a knock on the door.

Bert whipped the back of his hand across his mouth as if some guilty stain might be there. He called: 'Come in.'

Estelle had her back to the door and was busying herself with the tray when Con Bryer entered. Bert noticed that, like Estelle, Con wore beaded Indian-style moccasins. This was why neither of them had made a sound when coming along the passage.

Con looked from the girl to the man and back again. His dark eyes betokened absolutely nothing. The girl was half-turned towards him, but had not yet spoken, when he said: 'I didn't know you had company, Kid.'

'Miss Estelle was kind enough to bring me a meal.'

'That ain't exactly her job,' said Con, face and voice expressionless. He did not seem to be speaking to anybody in particular.

'Bucky an' the boy were both kinda busy,' said Estelle.

She placed the tray across Bert's lap, then left him. 'So-long, Kid,' she said. She passed Con and left the room. The door closed gently behind her. They did not hear her go away.

Con asked the Kid how he felt, and then also took himself off. Bert couldn't help wondering whether the boss's only reason for calling was to ask about his health. But he soon forgot the problem in attacking the meal Estelle had brought. Bucky was certainly a first-rate cook.

Not till afterwards did he think about Estelle. He had to admit she had stirred him. What kind of a woman was she? What did she want? Was she just a good-time girl buttering up to a big-shot like Con for what she could get out of it, or was she something else? She was young, voluptuous. She seemed full of devilment – even dangerous.

He looked up expectantly when the door was rapped again. But it was Bucky this time, padding in, asking after his condition and collecting the tray at the same time.

After that, the boys of the inner circle, all except Lenny the wrangler, came in one by one. Jack Tremaine stayed late to play a few hands of cards. Bert did not see Estelle again. The next day he was able to move about. The days passed quickly, and pretty soon he was downstairs once more, raring to go. All the boys had been taking it easy. No other jobs had been pulled while the Kid was laid up. There was a hue and cry about the bank job, but none of it seemed to be leading in this direction.

Entering the men's eating-place, Bert came face to face with Candy. He hesitated, then stuck out his hand. Candy took it. 'It was a good fight,' he said as they shook. Bert figured he might get to like Candy after all, now that the bad blood between them was washed away. Seemed like the only person now who did not accept the new member of the gang was Lenny the wrangler, and he didn't matter no more than a row of beans, anyway.

A little later Bert saw Estelle crossing the empty barroom. There was nobody else around. She had not seemed to notice him, so softly he called to her. When she turned towards him he saw that one side of her face was swollen and bruised. Before she could turn away again he caught up with her.

'Who did that?'

'Con. Who did you think?'

'Why?'

'Can't you guess why?' The next moment she had gone, leaving him standing there stupidly.

Then the rage came and he had to master it. When he was cooler he realized there was nothing he could do. He had liked Con. He would not like him anymore. For the rest – well, things would just continue to take their course.

The boys gathered in the messroom for the evening meal. A few of them had been out riding, reconnoitring. Tim Baggs had an item of news. Faro Creek had changed its name. It was now called Craddockville after its Mayor.

Everybody bellowed with laughter, the Kid most of all. 'What did I say?' he carolled. 'By gab, it seems too durned funny to be true.'

But when the Kid went to bed that night he was in a more sober mood. Mention of his home-town, even though it had changed its name, had brought back memories. Seemed like he had been kind of side-tracked from his original purpose in joining the Bryer gang. He figured it was time he took another look at 'Craddockville'.

He started out in darkness early the following morning and was careful to avoid being seen leaving Billstown. He knew what Con Bryer's feelings would be if he knew the Kid was returning to stick his head into the lion's mouth, even though the lion was more than likely to be asleep.

As dawn came he stood on the bare slopes of Boothill and looked down at the pitiful hump of the unmarked grave. And there they crept upon him, alone in his grief, and got him beneath their guns. A lone night-rider had seen him enter the town and had given him away. Six of them took him, rode him out on to the range and to bonds by a grove of execution. And as red slashed the sky the word went around. The ranchmen of Faro Creek (they would have no truck with fancy 'Craddockville' or Craddockville law) were about to dispense justice in their own way.

92

The girl heard of it only accidentally, for it had been purposely kept from her. The ranch was quiet, even her father had gone, surprisingly early for him. She moved quietly; she heard the cook and his garrulous assistant talking. She did not stop for coat or hat, but saddled her horse and rode like the wind.

The ranks of the watchers spread out so far that the arena seemed a mere speck by comparison. The arena which held the clump of cottonwoods, the hanging party and their victim. He had said very little and what he had said had gone unheard among the angry din of his would-be executioners. So he just sat there on his horse and looked about him, his eyes full of contempt and hate.

The girl burst through them. Bloodlusting though they were none of them dare lay a hand on a woman, particularly of one of the territory's greatest landowners, the girl whose father was one of the judges in the centre of that grim circle.

The rope was already around the young man's neck, a clenched quirt was uplifted above the horse's rump, when the girl burst into the inner circle. She reined in her horse so sharply that dust swirled. Her eyes were on him there above them, noting his bruised and bleeding face, his tattered clothing. They had been pretty rough in bringing him here; he had fought silently but with almost demoniacal strength despite the threat of their guns. They could have shot him; but they wanted to do things in a different way, to make an example of him that everybody in the pestilent Billstown would talk about – and beware!

She turned on them suddenly, her body tense with passion, her eyes blazing.

'You brutes! You filthy beasts!'

There was a gun in her hand too, though everybody had been too shocked by her sudden appearance to notice from whence she had drawn it. It was a Colt and looked huge in her small hand. She looked quite capable of shooting somebody with it. A man instinctively started forward to grab her.

An imperious voice said: 'Let her be,' and she half-turned in the saddle and saw her father.

She had known he would be there, but had been relieved at not having spotted him right away. She might have known that the revelation could not be put off: she had to accuse him the same as she had accused the others. The look in her eyes was enough, and the big man with the white hair seemed to shrink before it. She was his only daughter, the image of his dead wife, she had never looked at him before like that, he could not stand it.

She turned away from him and kneed her horse forward once more. She took the rope from around the young man's neck and nobody lifted a hand to stop her.

'Thanks, Miriam,' he said huskily.

The ring was still around them. There was no break, no escape. Simultaneously they seemed to realize this. The peril had not been stopped, only averted.

A man said: 'He's a murderous rustler. He must get his just deserts.'

It was a pompous pronouncement, but it found

favour. There were murmurs of assent, which the mob in the background echoed sullenly.

Things got swiftly more ugly. Men who would not have touched Miriam a few moments before seemed quite capable now of sweeping her out of the way and grabbing their prey once more. This metamorphosis was mainly due to the sudden collapse of their erstwhile leader, old Grosvenor, Miriam's father. Leadership was soon assumed by the old man's friend and neighbour, Jim Caldicott, who didn't have a daughter, anyway, and at that moment was mighty thankful for the fact. His own son was right there beside him ready, in fact, to wield the quirt that would send Bert Cave to perdition – once the noose was refitted, of course.

But another diversion occurred. The ranks broke once more and Mayor Craddock put in an appearance. What was more, accompanying him was 'Craddockville's' new sheriff, Lafe Cantell, and four hard-bitten deputies to boot.

Cantell already had quite a rep as a free-lance gunny when he was hired to ride law for the town. He brought his four deputies with him, hardcases like himself. All five of them were without a doubt the minions of the Craddock faction in town. More than ever now the ranchmen became aware of the cleavage between themselves and this faction.

Still, the law was the law, whether 'fixed' or not. There were six men here to back it up. You couldn't hang six lawmen.

So, after argument and narrowly averted gunplay, the prisoner was handed over. Mayor Craddock said he'd be tried as soon as possible. Mayor Craddock promised justice. A big trial would put Craddockville on the map, a guilty conviction even more so.

So the Kid was taken away. Away from the mob who had half-throttled him, away from the girl who had saved him.

He was incarcerated in the adobe jail. The same jail from which his father had been dragged by an angry mob and hanged, down by the livery stables. Things had been a little different then: the ranchmen had been in control, inside and outside of town. But the final result looked like being pretty much the same, anyway.

Maybe not quite the same though: the Kid figured he still had a slender chance. And why? Because on his way to the jail he had seen a man. That man had been leaning nonchalantly against a hitching-rail, smoking a cheroot. He had been alone, but even alone, and although he had given no sign, he radiated confidence to the young prisoner riding in the centre of a phalanx of lawmen. That man had been Tim Baggs of Laredo. Tim with the quick trigger and the devil-may-care ice-cold nerves.

Where was Tim now? the Kid wondered. On his way back to Billstown to give out with the news? Or maybe not?

Even if he had gone back to Billstown and given Con Bryer the news, would Con do anything about it or would the Kid hang, out of mind? Wouldn't he be scared that the Kid would talk, or would he, gambler and student of human nature that he was, take it for granted that the Kid would not talk no matter what they did to him?

The Kid, languishing in his cell, suddenly became less optimistic. He didn't know what to think. His father had had friends. And now Bert Cave was back in the past again, remembering what his father's friends had done for him. Public opinion, the new and powerful public opinion of Faro Creek had alleged that Jonathon Cave had rustled his neighbour's cattle and killed one of his neighbour's hands, a popular cuss, a singing night-rider known as 'Melody' Jinks. The evidence had been circumstantial, but pretty damning. Some of Jim Caldicott's cattle had been found among Jonathon's meagre herd. Brands had been clumsily blotted. Two cowpunchers who worked for another neighbour, Cal Grosvenor, Miriam's father, stated they had seen Jonathon riding away like the wind. And only five minutes before they found the bullet-ridden body of 'Melody', his guitar smashed and bloodstained beneath him.

Anyway, the big ones said, what could you expect from a nester, a sod-buster? – which was all Jonathon Cave was. He and his little spread had been a thorn in the side of the cattle barons for a long time. They had tried to buy him out, and couldn't. So they had harassed him. Maybe they had pushed him too far and, like a cornered rat, he had turned and struck.

He had friends, small men like himself: they were vociferous in their conviction of his innocence, but they did not try to save him. Maybe they were not to be blamed: they had been outnumbered four to one and all of them had families to consider – whereas Jonathon, a widower, had only his son, Bert. It had all been over when Bert got to town. He had tried to shoot Jim Caldicott there on the main street and had been seized and clapped in a cell. But the town's bloodlust had already been satiated, they were quiet now, they had made their hypocritical gesture. The following morning they let Bert cut his father's body down; some of them helped him to bury it on Boothill. Then, as Jonathon's property had already been confiscated, his son was banished from Faro Creek (now 'Craddockville') and told never to return.

And so, the wheel had come full circle now, and it looked like the Caves, father and son, were losers every time.

CHAPTER 9

There were plenty of the Caldicott and Grosvenor faction in town that night. And plenty of talk of doing the same to Bert Cave as had been done to his father, the sooner the last of the breed was out of the way, the better. Bert Cave was an owlhooter, he had been seen riding with rustlers that stormy night when three good Caldicott men had been killed. There was only one judgment that could be possible; why wait for a trial just because fat Craddock and his pet lawmen said so? The trial would be only a mockery, anyway.

The Kid in his cell heard the sullen rumbling. The shouted threats as the more youthful and useless of his enemies, the sort who would be right at the back if trouble really started, lurched past the jail.

Lafe Cantell heard it all too, and smiled thinly and cruelly. He was a tall man, painfully thin, with predatory features, fish-like eyes and thin, greying hair. He looked as if all the better human emotions had been drained out of his body long since, leaving only skin and bone and hate and cruelty. If Lafe had any good human emotions at all it was that of courage.

He cared for his guns far more than he cared for anything of flesh and blood. He loved trouble. Sometimes it seemed to his men that he had suicidal tendencies; he invited trouble with total disregard for odds or circumstances. He was a wild and supreme gambler and didn't even seem aware of the fact.

He had sent three of his men out into the town with orders to report to him if things got too ugly. He was willing to fight the whole town if need be. Not because he liked his prisoner, or had any strong sense of duty, but because he hated anybody to get the better of him. Courage, cruelty and pride: yes, he had all those emotions, if they could be called that.

His men were not so keen to invite trouble as he was, but they were not crazy enough to say so. Any man who disagreed with Lafe was liable to find himself forced into a gun duel. Probably with fatal results, for Lafe was pretty fast.

Besides, his men told themselves and each other, there were rich pickings here, playing the town against the ranchers, and vice-versa. Lafe wouldn't take on a clean-up job like this unless there was plenty of dinero involved, though Lafe didn't seem to bother about the money for himself, he seldom spent any. He smoked and drank very sparingly; he wore his clothes until they dropped off him. Only his gunbelt and twin guns were well cared for. They were good and old and well-worn. The guns were well-oiled and they bore their notches bravely in their scarred walnut butts.

His two remaining men helped to guard the jail. One was on the front porch, the other outside the back door, the door which led into the cell-block. Lafe sat in the office, lolling back in the swivel-chair with his feet up on the desk. He still wore his gunbelt, he had it in a comfortable position. His long arms hung over the sides of the chair, his sleeves brushing the butts of his guns. He was indolent, yet he might have been carved from stone. He did not smoke, he did not move. He sat and looked into space, with his little eyes half-closed, and listened to the murmur of the would-be judges and executioners down there on the Main Street. His lips were a little twisted, but he was not smiling.

He heard the soft whistling of his side-kick in the porch, and then the sound was stilled. He heard the soft thud as of something falling and, when the door opened, he was standing, a gun in each hand.

'Welcome, Tim,' he said.

Tim Baggs blinked a little in the light. He had a gun in his hand, but he held it by the barrel, for he had slugged the guard with the other end. He grinned crookedly, the livid scar twisting in his lean face.

'Howdy, Lafe,' he said. 'We meet again. And you don't seem surprised to see me.'

'I spotted you in the street this morning. I could hardly believe my eyes at first. 1 thought you had been driven plumb into the Atlantic Ocean before now.'

'All the tinpot lawmen in the West – yourself included – couldn't drive me into the ocean,' said Tim Baggs laconically.

101

'The young hellion in the cell – is he your friend?'

'Kind of.'

'I figured that. You are of the same kind.'

'Does a tin star make a man better?' said the man from Laredo. 'You've always sold your guns to the highest bidder. Sheriff of Craddockville. Pah!' His grin widened. Then ignoring the levelled guns he spat on the floor between himself and the lawman.

Lafe Cantell's little eyes sparked: his pride had been hurt.

'Drop the gun, Tim,' he said. 'Then you can go an' join your friend in the cell.'

'I always said you and I would meet again, Lafe,' said the scarfaced man. 'That day on the street of Laredo I said we'd meet again. You had two of your rats with you then – you drove me out like a dog.'

'We could have killed you. Nobody would've complained.'

'I would rather have been killed than shamed,' said Tim Baggs softly. 'You knew that. We are very much alike, you and I, Lafe.'

'You haven't dropped your gun yet, Tim,' said Lafe. 'I have no more time to argue. Do as you're told or I'll shoot you where you stand.'

Tim Baggs had courage too. He remained as he was, the gun still dangling in his hand. 'You always were afraid of me, Lafe,' he said almost in a whisper. 'You've always had the inside edge. Last time you had two men to help you. This time you have the drop on me with two guns. You could've shot me down as I entered, but your pride wouldn't let you – I knew that. We're both outlaws. But you won't admit you're

102

an outlaw. You see in me a reflection of yourself. You also think that if the test came I might, avowed outlaw though I am, prove the better man. Because of this you're afraid of me.'

'You always have been a fancy talker,' sneered Lafe, but his little eyes were hot now. 'You know I've never been afraid of anything,' he added softly.

'Holster your guns then an' give me an even break.'

The words fell like stones in the silent room. The men had been talking softly. Nobody outside of that room could have heard them. Now the silence was absolute. Tim Baggs would have made a great gambler. He knew his man, he played his last card against him and he staked everything on it.

The seconds ticked away. Then Lafe Cantell slowly lowered his guns. 'Goddam you,' he said. 'We'll have this out right now. A finish – a finish!' He was suddenly far more passionate than was his wont.

His guns were sheathed. Tim spun his own gun, dipped it into its holster. But Lafe was moving again already, and Tim threw himself swiftly to one side. Yeah, Lafe had courage, but he liked the inside edge sometimes too.

The gunfire was hideous in the enclosed space. Blue smoke swirled. For one of the first times in his life Lafe Cantell was suddenly scared and inadequate. He died realizing it.

The grinning Tim Baggs steadied himself with one hand against the wall. He turned his head to glance at the bullet hole in the wall a few inches to his left.

Then he was moving swiftly, bending behind the desk to scoop up one of the fallen man's guns. He was straightening up when Lafe's side-kick charged in from the back passage. He turned, jerking his gun up. Tim Baggs shot him in the face with his boss's own Colt, then leapt over the body, calling: 'Kid! Kid!'

'Here, Tim, here!'

The man from Laredo had not bothered to look for keys. He blew the lock apart with two well-placed shots. He handed the spare gun to Bert.

'Let's get moving before we have the whole town about our ears. I've got your horse out back, along with my own.'

They strode over the recumbent form of the rear guard. Tim had taken no chances, except with Lafe, and maybe even that had been a foregone conclusion too.

The two men mounted. They heard the growing din in Main Street as they thundered away across the range.

They almost ran into a lone rider who came thundering in the opposite direction. The scarfaced man was drawing his gun when Bert shouted: 'Hold it, Tim! It's my friend, Miriam. She saved my life this morning.'

'You're free!' the girl gasped. 'I would've tried to let you free. I must see you, Bert – I must tell you—'

She was almost incoherent. The wind tossed her words away from her crazily. From behind the little group now came the sounds of pursuit.

'You must go, Miriam,' bawled Bert. 'You mustn't

be seen with us. You've done so much. The mob are crazy now.'

'But Bert. I must—'

'Go,' he almost screamed. 'Go!' He raised his fist. For a moment it seemed he would strike her. But instead, he brought his knuckles down hard on her horse's rump. The beast snorted, whirled, streaked homewards. The two men went off at a tangent, riding madly, the wind whipping at them.

When finally they halted to listen, all they could hear was the wind. 'I hope they didn't follow the girl by mistake,' said Bert.

CHAPTER 10

The gang was sitting pretty, they could all afford to rest up while the law of Aceville, with countless reinforcements, chased its tail looking for bank robbers. However, Con suddenly changed his mind about the duration of the gang's 'holiday'. One of his boys had been manhandled, almost killed. The perpetrators of this outrage must be punished. Anyway, it was time the landowners of Craddockville were harassed once more; it was time the boys of Billstown wiped out the memory of the farce that had attended their last visit to that hated territory.

Privately, Bert Cave figured it was a little too early to attack Craddock territory again, but he kept his mouth shut. If Con wanted to have another smack at those coyotes, here was one member of his gang who was raring to go.

Con sent a couple of men out there to reconnoitre, first of all. He told the rest of the bunch to stand by, not on any account to leave town. They drank, ate, played cards. Bert put in some more target practice with Jack Tremaine. He was improving quickly. Once more Jack told him he was a born gunfighter. Some more of the boys joined in, and Bert watched them and began to realize just how good he could be, better than all of them someday, maybe.

But did he want to be a gunfighter? Did he want to make a rep for himself the way Jack Tremaine had done? What had Jack got out of it all? Money? But where to spend it? Having to be on the alert all the time, lawmen after his scalp; his own kind too, some of them avid to gain the doubtful honour of being the one to cut down 'the fastest gun in the West' – and so on, to their own fame and probably their own early death. And so it went on, a vicious circle. No wonder Jack looked kind of sad and bewildered sometimes. Did Bert want that?

Whether or not, he did want to learn to shoot straight and fast. He had some 'cutting-down' to do himself, if somebody else didn't cut him down first.

He was still feeling kind of battered after the rough handling he had received at Craddockville, so after lunch he went up to his room to lie down.

He drew the curtains to keep out the sunshine. He was dozing when he heard the soft footsteps in the passage. Then his door was rapped.

His hand moved nearer to the gun on the chair beside the bed. He called, 'Come in.'

It was Estelle May. He had half-expected this. He cursed himself for the effect this filly always had on him.

He sat up on the bed. She closed the door softly behind her. 'Bert.' Her voice was a little breathless. It was the first time she had called him anything other than 'handsome'. 'I heard you had been in the wars again. Are you all right now?' She gave a little giggle. She seemed as nervous as he was, which was quite a change for her.

He swung his body around and let his stockinged feet fall to the floor. He had been lying on top of the bed in shirt and trousers. He said: 'I'm fine now, thanks, Estelle. How've you been?'

'About the same, I guess.'

The conversation was banal. He wondered if she was thinking the same as he was thinking. She was peering at him in the semi-darkness. He saw that she was wearing one of the tight-fitting, low-cut backless gowns which were her bar-room uniform. For some obscure reason this fact made him savage.

She came nearer to the bed. With a practised sway now. She didn't talk anymore. Maybe she wasn't nervous any more, anyway.

He stood up, turned to reach for the curtains.

'Don't open those,' she said softly. No, she wasn't nervous any more.

He let his hands fall and turned towards her.

The footsteps outside were very sudden. Then the door was flung open. Light streamed in from the passage. Con Bryer came in swiftly as the girl stepped away from Bert.

'I thought I'd find you here,' he said. But he went past her and advanced on Bert. The latter could not see his face very clearly – Con's back was to the light – but he could tell by the tenseness of the lean body that the boss was in one of his quiet, killing passions.

Con raised his hand. Bert got ready to cover up,

strike out. He had seen the boss slap men's faces. But no man must do that to Bert Cave.

His gun was behind him. He could not have reached it quickly enough. Even if it had been at his hip he could not have beaten Con's draw. Con had dropped his hand; even before Bert had divined his intention the gun was there.

A ball of ice formed in the Kid's stomach. He tensed himself against the blast of the slugs.

'Con!' said Estelle. 'Don't! Don't!'

He did not move a muscle. 'Get out of here, you!' he said. His voice was as expressionless as if he had been calling his hand at cards.

She cursed him then, poured the invective out at his unheeding back. Bert Cave momentarily forgot his peril. Despite his youth, he was tough and hard and cynical. But he was shocked now by the things Estelle said, by the words she used. He had never thought to hear such things from a woman's lips, particularly so young a woman as Estelle May. She was no longer sweet.

She moved nearer to Con, lashing him with her tongue. He did not flinch. 'Get away from me,' he said, 'or, by God, I'll drop this young puppy where he stands.'

She did not look at Bert again. She spun on her heels and flounced from the room. As she moved into the passage she started to laugh harshly. Then the slammed door cut off the mocking sound.

Bert had contemplated jumping Con, but the boss had not moved a muscle. There had been no chance, and now Bert felt kind of sick. Was he to cash in his chips now in this shameful way and all through a shallow good-time dance-hall bit! He thought of Miriam. He would have liked to see Miriam just once more.

Con was playing with him like a cat playing with a mouse. Con liked that.

Bert Cave resolved that if die he must, he would die like a tiger, not like a sitting dog. Maybe he could even take this skunk's scalp with him as he went.

But it was almost as if Con Bryer read his mind. `Don't try anything, Kid,' he said, 'or I'll shoot you in the stomach. Have you ever seen a man die with a bullet in the stomach, Kid? It's slow, and very painful.'

'Have your fun,' said the Kid.

'I've had it! You didn't really think I would shoot you because of that trollop, do you? It was inevitable that she'd set her cap at you. I'll turn her out.' The boss lowered his gun.

Bert still thought there was a catch in it. He knew that Con was quite capable of killing any man who injured his pride. It would be so easy to jerk that gun up again.

But Con was already turning away. He made one last remark before leaving the room. 'Don't try and see her before she goes.'

'I won't,' said Bert. He never wanted to see Estelle again. He felt ashamed and deflated. Estelle had made a fool of him. Also in a subtle way, Con had made a fool of him too. Was Con just biding his time; had he, while holding the gun, started to plan a more subtle revenge?

111

Bert had liked Con. Now he found himself hating him. He wished he had never joined up with Con, had gone on to accomplish his mission alone, even if he died in the attempt. Now he was being hedged round by restrictions and was liable to get a bullet in the back, ultimately, just the same. He discovered that he hated Con far more than he had hated Candy Sampson, whom he didn't hate anymore. He knew somehow that he had to hate Con now, watch Con constantly.

He could not lie in his room any more. He put on his boots swiftly and crossed the room. As he hit the passage, Lenny the wrangler was coming out of the bathroom. He leered impudently at the Kid as he passed. The Kid had an idea that Lenny had heard what had gone on in the room. He hated Lenny too. But he knew no use would be served by challenging the little rat now.

He went downstairs. Bucky, busy polishing glasses, greeted him from behind the bar. Con and Estelle were nowhere around. Lenny had gone to earth some place again. The bar-room was empty except for Candy Sampson playing patience at a table in the corner. He inclined his head, made a gesture. Bert joined him. Candy still bore the mark of his fists, but didn't seem to be holding it against him. They went on playing. Tim Baggs and Jack Tremaine joined them presently and made up a foursome.

Dusk began to creep into the room. Bucky yelled 'Come an' pit it' and they left their cards for a while and filed into the messroom for the slap-up feed that was always provided at this time. They might have

112

been cowhands returning for chow after a hard day's work; except that no cowhand ate grub quite as fine as this.

The boss did not put in an appearance. Sometimes he took his meals in his room; but the boys knew better than to pump Bucky about this. Maybe the boss was off on one of his mysterious rides.

Bert Cave began to wonder about Estelle. Although he had nothing but contempt for that filly now, he hoped Con had not manhandled her, or hadn't planned an exit even more subtle and terrible.

The two boys returned from reconnoitring Craddockville territory. Things seemed pretty quiet there, they said. At least there were no signs that any of the ranches, or the town itself, had been turned into fortresses.

'That'll please Con,' said Jack Tremaine.

'Hadn't you better go report to him, Jack?' suggested Candy. 'Maybe he'll want us to ride tonight.'

'I doubt it,' said Jack. He did not make a move to act on Candy's suggestion.

Another absentee from the supper-table was Lenny the wrangler, but Lenny was such an unpopular little rat that nobody had remarked about his absence. Now, as there was an altercation from the direction of the bar-room, folks recognized Lenny's voice. Finally Lenny burst into the room with Bucky close behind.

Bucky said: 'You oughta go an' put your head under the pump.'

'I'm all right,' said Lenny. But his voice was thick, his eyes bleary, his gait unsteady. 'Bring me some grub!' he shouted.

Bucky shrugged good-humouredly and returned to the kitchen. Lenny plumped himself at the table and looked about him owlishly, but with the usual malice in his little eyes. He almost seemed to be licking his lips – as if he had some great revelation to impart yet didn't mean to do so unless somebody questioned him. It was a change for him to be the cynosure of all eyes. It made him feel important. He made the most of it.

'What made you get into that state?' said Jack Tremaine. 'The boss's orders were for us all to go easy tonight.'

Lenny winked evilly. 'I've seen the boss,' he said.

Jack ignored this, went on: 'An' you had to go somewhere else to get it, didn't you? Bucky wouldn't have served you with that much.'

'Yuh durn' tootin' he wouldn't,' said Bucky himself, who had just entered. He planked a heaped steaming plate before Lenny. 'I hope it chokes you,' he added conversationally.

'Go back to your fry-pen, you fat freak,' said Lenny loftily.

Bucky raised his hand as if he would drive the wrangler's face into the steaming mixture beneath. But a look from Jack stayed him, and he grinned, turned and left the room.

'What made you act the goat in this way?' said Jack. 'If Con was here there'd be trouble, an' you know it.'

'Con ain't here,' said Lenny. 'I knew he wouldn't

114

be here. Now shut your face an' let me eat my meal before it get's cold.'

Scared looks were thrown at Jack. Nobody there had ever spoken to him like that, except in jest; and Lenny hadn't been joking. The particular snake-poison he had imbibed must be really something!

But Jack humoured the drunkard. 'I want an explanation,' he said. 'Maybe when you've eaten, your brain'll be clearer. I'll wait. You better compensate me for my waiting. It better be good, pardner.'

The implied threat was plain to everybody except, it seemed, the one at whom it was aimed. Maybe he was too drunk to notice, or too hungry; he was attacking the meal as if his life depended on it. It would have been better had he taken his time over it, thus prolonging his life a little more.

Many of the men had risen to leave the room, but without exception they seated themselves again. They were willing to wait too. It might be worth waiting for. Whatever it was. The bar-room was filling up with evening customers. Their voices were heard, their laughter, the stamping of their heavy riding boots. The girls had come down too and were greeting the suckers. Somebody began to play the piano. A raucous voice called: 'Hallo, honey-pot!' A girl screamed with laughter. Somebody was thumping on the bar with a fist in time to the music that somebody else was murdering.

'Shut that door,' said Jack Tremaine to nobody in particular.

Candy Sampson was nearest. He obeyed the order without one of his usual impertinent comments.

Lenny was swigging coffee, pausing every now and then to leer at anybody who happened to catch his eye. Once he caught the Kid's glance and the look changed to one of hate. Bert realized that ever since that first night, when he had plugged the little wrangler, Lenny had hated him, was only biding his time in order to pay him back. Lenny was a killer, but he wanted the inside edge first.

The Kid forgot about Lenny, however, as a female voice squealed at the other side of the door. He caught himself listening for one particular voice. He had not heard it, and was not likely to now the door was closed. He wondered whether Estelle was in there or whether Con had already sent her packing. How would she leave? There was no stage and it would be a rough ride for a woman on horseback. Not that that would weigh anything with Con: he was quite capable of making her walk if it amused him to do so. Where was Con, anyway?

Lenny mopped his plate clean with bread and shoved the last morsel into his mouth. Then he reached across the table for the wedge of apple pie that was left in the dish and began to champ on that. When that was finished he rose to his feet and bellowed: 'I want some more coffee!' He lurched across the room towards the door. 'Where in hell's that fat freak?'

'Come back here an' sit down,' said Jack Tremaine. There was something in his voice that stopped the drunken man in his tracks. He turned and, blinking owlishly, returned to his seat. Maybe he wasn't quite so drunk now. Maybe he had never been as drunk as he pretended to be. But a new sense of his own importance had gone to his head more quickly than wine and, foolishly ignoring the danger signs, he was playing to the gallery for all he was worth.

'So you've seen the boss,' barked Jack. 'Did the boss give you permission to go an' make a jackass of yourself.'

'I didn't ask him. He didn't see me. But I saw him. And his lady-friend, that filly, Estelle May.'

'Is there anything strange in that?'

'They wuz going ridin',' leered Lenny 'They don't usually go ridin' at night.'

Candy Sampson guffawed suddenly. 'Lenny's jealous. He always fancied his arm with that filly. He'd like to cut the boss out. I reckon that after he seed them, hobnobbing like a coupla lovebirds, he went an' drowned his sorrows in drink.'

Lenny shot the young man a murderous glance. Evidently there was some truth in what Candy had said. The first part of it, anyway; though the thought of the ratlike Lenny with the young and voluptuous Estelle was kind of ludicrous.

Jack Tremaine quelled Candy with a glance, addressed Lenny once more. 'I don't know what you're getting at, yuh loony little skunk, but go on.'

'They looked like they wuz goin' on a nice long ride,' said Lenny. 'I figured that if my boss could go lollygaggin' across country with his lady friend, I wuz entitled to get myself a few li'l drinks. So I went an' got me a few li'l drinks.'

'You did, huh?' said Jack. 'Wal, now I'm gonna ask

three of the boys to take you outside an' hold you under the pump. Grado – Tim – Candy—'

Lenny sprang to his feet. 'Wait a minute!' His expression was so murderous that, despite themselves, the three men were brought up short. Jack did not urge them on. This was a kind of a new Lenny. Jack wanted to see which way the little polecat would jump next.

CHAPTER 11

Lenny held the centre of the stage again. But now he realized he might have overstepped the mark and he had to talk fast.

'Estelle May had a bundle with her. She looked like she wouldn't be coming back.'

'Now he's grieving,' said Candy Sampson, but he failed to raise a laugh this time.

'An' I know why she won't be comin' back,' burst out Lenny. 'She was locked in the Kid's room with him.' He pointed a finger dramatically at Bert Cave. 'And the boss caught 'em there.'

Bert sprang to his feet. 'It's a lie. The door wasn't locked. Estelle just came in to ask me if I was better after the beating I had got in Craddockville.'

But Lenny went on, pell-mell. 'Con threatened to shoot the Kid. The Kid would've been a goner now if Estelle hadn't pleaded for his life. I told you all along the Kid's a jinx an' a troublemaker. Candy said the Kid was a jinx all along.' He looked at Candy for confirmation, but Candy gave no sign, did not speak.

'The Kid's a troublemaker. I don't trust him. He's

119

out to get us all—' Lenny screamed on, throwing insults at Bert Cave. He was almost incoherent now. He didn't seem to know what he was saying.

The Kid realized Lenny must have been listening in to his stack-up with Con. He realized also that the fact that Estelle had set her cap at him (Bert) when she wouldn't give the ugly little wrangler a second look had been another score Lenny could chalk up, swelling his hymn of hate. It was all coming out now, and Bert knew he must stop it before Lenny's over-riding hate was communicated to these other men.

'Stop it,' he bawled. 'Stop it!'

He might have been shouting into the wind for all the effect his words had. Lenny looked on the point of foaming at the mouth. He screamed fantastic accusations as he tried to bring the other men on to his side.

Bert skirted the table. He swung his arm and gave Lenny a ringing slap across the face with his open palm. Lenny staggered back, his flood of words dammed. 'You're a filthy, stinking liar,' said Bert through set teeth, looming over him.

Lenny snarled like a trapped animal and reached for his gun.

Bert's action was purely instinctive, the way Jack had taught him, brain and eye and muscle coordi-nated. He fired from the hip. Lenny took the slug in the left shoulder. He gave a choking cry and stag-gered, flapping ungainly. He went over on his back, his head flopping back against the wall. He levered himself up into a sitting position, his face a mask of hate and agony. His gun was still in his hand. He raised it.

'Kid!' shouted Jack Tremaine.

Bert knew it was Lenny's life or his. He jerked himself to one side as he fired again, but his gunhand was as steady as a rock. He felt the hot breath of the bullet going past his face; his own slug hit Lenny in the chest, slamming him back against the wall once more. He slid down it, finished up; this time he lay still.

Almost mechanically the Kid holstered his smoking gun and turned away. The door flew open and a couple of nosey townsfolk burst in. Jack Tremaine's gun was in his hand then. He said one word, 'Out', and the two men fled. Tim Baggs shut the door behind them.

'Wal, I guess the little rat had it comin' to him,' said Jack.

'Yeah?' said Tim Baggs, laconic as ever.

Nobody else spoke. Bert Cave wondered what the reactions of the other men would have been had not Jack taken the lead and pointed their way for them. Tim Baggs would probably have turned up trumps, anyway – but Candy Sampson, Grado Bear, Med Jones—?'

The latter was examining Lenny now. But the verdict was a foregone conclusion. Lenny would break no more horses, tell no more lies, covet no more pretty girls.

The door opened again and Bucky slid his huge body through the aperture and closed it behind him. He took in the scene in a glance which gave nothing away. 'My, my,' he said tonelessly. 'Bloodshed. You, Kid?'

The Kid nodded.

'I could see it boilin' up,' said Bucky. 'It had to be one of you sooner or later.' He didn't add whether he was pleased with the final count or not; but the tension was lifted.

The body was laid out in a back room, safe from prying eyes. Jack went in search of Con in order to report. It was just a gesture: he did not find Con.

Bert Cave elected to go for a walk, alone. He figured that if anybody was keen to avenge Lenny's death they might as well make their play now as later. He would be walking the street alone. Jack seemed to understand. He watched the Kid until the dark bend of the main street hid him completely.

Bert walked to the end of town and back again. His direction was not purposeful, he almost meandered. He broke his pasear on the way back to take a couple of drinks in a cantina. Nobody spoke to him. Nobody seemed to know that a man had recently been killed at the other end of the street. Still, this was Billstown.

Some time later he passed a dark alley. He had passed the same alley twice before. Now a soft voice called his name. He whirled, his hand going to his gun. Was this it? But the voice called again, and he knew for sure this time that it was a woman's voice.

He was not sure what he had expected to find.

'Miriam! Why—?'

'Hush! Bert, please, I—'

Her words broke off with a sob, and the next moment she was in his arms, her head on his chest. He could feel her soft body quivering beneath his hands.

'Miriam, you shouldn't be here,' he hissed. 'Of all the crazy things.'

Her muffled voice came to him. 'You don't understand.'

'But I do. I've missed you, Miriam. But—'

She clutched his arm with such force that he winced. His words were stemmed. She spoke again, drawing away from him a little. She had gotten a hold of herself again.

'Bert. It's father. He's been shot. The – the doctor doesn't expect him to live—'

'Who did it?'

'We don't know. He was dry-gulched while he was out riding. He was alone.'

'Why should—?'

But as if she realized what he meant to say, though it was forced from him, she cut in again. 'He wants to see you, Bert. We might not have much time.'

'Did he send you, send his only daughter to this hellhole?'

'No, he didn't. He didn't seem to think it would ever be possible to see you again – although he so badly wants to.

'How do I know it's not some kind of trap he's trying to spring?'

'Bert, would I—?'

He grabbed her. 'Quiet!'

The footsteps went by, close to the end of the alley, and faded away on the boardwalk. From the distance came the sound of revelry.

'I'm sorry for what I said,' whispered Bert. He continued to hold her.

'You can't be blamed for thinking as you do,' said Miriam. 'I am ashamed that anyone bearing my name should've—'

'Forget it,' said Bert sharply. 'What does your Dad want to see me about?'

'I'm not sure – but I think it's to do with your father.'

'Where's your horse?'

'At the end of the alley.'

'C'mon then, I'll go get mine.'

A few minutes later they were riding away from Billstown. Bert knew what the boys would think of him. They would think he had run because of possible vengeance on the part of Lenny's friends, or even because he feared the boss's wrath. But he realized he didn't much care what the boys thought, except maybe Jack Tremaine and Tim Baggs. Still, it couldn't be helped.

The young man and the girl wasted no more time talking. In fact, they wouldn't have been able to talk, for they rode at a breakneck gallop, the wind whipping at them furiously. The night was dark and the range floor uneven. The ride was dangerous, but they had both been almost born in the saddle and they did not think of danger, only of reaching a dying man before it was too late.

Bert Cave's mind was a little confused. Was this ride to lead him finally to the end of his quest, his vengeance? In joining up with Con Bryer and his gang had he taken a false step, and was it too late to turn back? He could not conjecture why Cal Grosvenor wanted to see him so desperately. Dark suspicions clouded his mind; then were sent skittling by wild, optimistic surmises.

The ride, in places, had something of the quality of a nightmare. Yet Bert Cave could not help being reminded of other rides he had taken with this girl by his side, so many of them, stretching back through the years. When he had been a lanky kid in ragged jeans and she a bouncing tomboy, pigtails streaming in the wind. They had been good times. This reckless ride was so very similar to so many others taken by night and by day, yet there was so much different too, both in his relationship with Miriam and in other things. He felt no cynicism now about his feelings for Miriam, he realized he must've been fighting them unconsciously all the time, ever since she met him on the trail after he was driven from Faro Creek, and he knew she was no longer a child, but a beautiful and desirable young woman. Miriam had known of this thing between them all along and she had not tried to fight it. He was overjoyed to think that this was so. But where did it leave an outlaw like him in relation to her, daughter of a rich landowner? And the pessimistic gloom settled over him once more.

They hit the secondary trail which wound within a few miles of Craddockville, speared on into the range then, a couple of miles outside the town broke into two separate tracks, one to the Grosvenor Ranch, the other to Jim Caldicott's place. A jumbled outcrop of boulders marked this junction.

The wind had dropped a little now, so that the horses, though still travelling pretty fast, did not have to struggle against it. The night was still fairly dark;

there was no moon, but tiny pin-points of stars were struggling through, giving the range an eerie light. The two riders slowed a little as they approached the outcrop of rocks, for here they had to fork sharply right.

Bert Cave saw the glint of starlight on steel there in the rocks, and even as the two men came into view he was shouting a warning to Miriam, veering his horse off the trail, covering her. He was drawing his gun at the same time, elevating it towards the shapeless faces. A slug took his hat off. His horse shied. He left the saddle, half-jumping, half-tumbling. The night was full of gunfire. He had a confused glimpse of Miriam. She had a gun in her hand too, and somehow that did not seem very surprising. He almost fell on his back, but managed to right himself. He dropped on one knee. The two attackers had been thrown off-stride by his tumble from his horse. They were close together, trying to calm their own skittish mounts and get a bead on their quarry at the same time.

A gun barked from behind Bert and one of the riders lost his hat. Then Bert was fanning the hammer of his own Colt, reflecting cynically how many cans he would've been able to fetch off the fence with that barrage. The targets were much bigger this time; they tumbled from their perches like ripe falling fruit. One lay still. The other lurched to his feet, triggering savagely. Bert winced as a slug burned his arm. Then he cut his man down, watched him crumple into immobility.

There was a stillness in both those figures now, a stillness that would not change. The rocks squatted lumpishly in the pale starlight. There was no more danger from that direction. The night was quiet again. Bert turned, and as he did so, Miriam came up to him. Her gun, a Colt as big as Bert's own, still dangled from her small fist. But she sheathed it now and gripped his arm. It was a brief and simple gesture, but it meant quite a lot.

Bert moved over to the two still figures, and she followed him. With him she bent over them and he did not find anything strange in that. She was no prissy little city girl who might pass out at the sight of blood. Luckily, neither of the two men had been hit in the face or head. They both had their kerchiefs pulled up so that their faces were masked, only their eyes and a narrow strip of brow revealed beneath their turned-down hat brims. This was the strange facelessness that Bert had noticed about them in their sudden appearance. But now he tore the cloth away and they were faceless no longer.

'Two of Jim Caldicott's men,' said Miriam quietly.

'Yeah.' Bert recognized them too as a couple of Caldicott's oldest hands; both of them had had a pretty fast rep.

'Maybe they were guarding the trail in case any of your friends from Billstown paid us a visit.'

'Then why would they be masked? There was no need for them to disguise themselves from anybody from Billstown. They'd only need to disguise themselves from somebody who knew them, from you for instance.'

'You think they were waiting for me, or for both of us?'

'I think they knew – or guessed – that you'd be coming back this way and that maybe you'd have somebody with you.'

'I didn't think anybody knew where I was going.'

'Maybe somebody tailed you part of the way – or somebody told them where you might be going.'

The full significance of his last words seemed to be lost on the girl. She made a little helpless gesture. 'But why would these two men want to harm me?'

'Maybe it wasn't you they wanted to harm,' retorted Bert. He was sick at heart. 'Maybe they just wanted whoever was riding with you. That was why they were masked, so that you wouldn't recognize who had done the job.'

'It's all very puzzling,' said Miriam. She made that little ineffectual gesture again. 'But we're wasting time – we're wasting time, Bert.'

He dragged the two bodies behind the rocks. He slapped the horses on their rumps and sent them galloping away. He knew that they would go straight home and the killing of the two Caldicott men would soon be discovered. He knew that he was burning his bridges behind him, but that didn't seem to matter any more now. He had never killed a man until today, and now in the space of a few hours he had put check on three. He felt that he never wanted to kill again, no matter in what cause. But he had an idea he would not be allowed for very long to adhere to that admirable resolution.

He remounted his horse. Man and girl rode onwards silently.

CHAPTER 12

They did not meet anyone else. They heard the lowing of cattle in the distance. Then they topped a rise, and the ranch buildings lay beneath them, drowsing in the pale starlight. Down there a dog barked mournfully. There was something lost and lonely about the sound. The man and the girl urged their horses at a gallop down the hill.

The corral gate was swinging as they approached it. The dog was barking more shrilly now as if something had startled it. Maybe it had gotten wind of their approach. A voice yelled at it to 'Shut up', and it became silent.

Bert caught the rein of Miriam's horse and brought the beast to a standstill beside his own.

'There's somebody in the corral.' His gun was in his hand as he dismounted.

The figure appeared at the rail then, a few yards away from the gate. It was inside the corral. It was harmless too, hanging over the top of the rail like a limp rag, it's arms on the other side, its hands making little supplicating gestures in the direction of the two people.

A name burst involuntarily from Bert's lips. Then he was running to the corral gate, swinging it open. He heard Miriam move behind, heard the pattering of her feet. The other woman, for woman it undoubtedly was, turned her body around but still held desperately on to the fence until he reached her, and then she gave a little mewing cry and let herself fall slackly into his arms. When Miriam reached them he was lowering her gently to the ground, letting himself go with her, her head resting on his knee.

'Who is it, Bert?'

'A girl from Billstown. A girl called Estelle. She was Con Bryer's girl.'

'Oh, the poor thing. Is she badly hurt?'

'I don't know yet.'

Estelle was making little pitiful sounds, trying to talk.

'Take it easy, *chiquita*,' he said, the Spanish endearment coming easily, almost flippantly, to his lips.

He straightened up with her cradled in his arms. 'Where can I take her?'

'Up to my room.'

Miriam led the way, taking the horses with her. A man came out of the bunkhouse as they neared it. His manner was suspicious, pugnacious. Miriam accosted him, spoke a few soft words. He turned, retraced his steps.

Miriam left the horses at a small tie-rail then led the way through the side door of the ranch-house, a large, bungalow-type building with a verandah all round. A light burned in the passage. There was no sound.

A door opened and a man came through. Bert recognized Doc Mackey from Faro Creek. The elderly whitehaired man showed no surprise at seeing him there. He shook his head slowly from side to side.

'We're too late,' breathed Miriam. She faltered in her stride momentarily, then squared her shoulders and carried on. 'We've got another patient for you, doctor.'

The old mossy-horn certainly wasn't easy to surprise. Without comment he fell in with the cavalcade. He was a bustling little man. Behind them Bert heard a door open again. Involuntarily he turned his head. Here now came another Faro Creek (Craddockville) worthy, Perry Cloony, the lawyer. He saw Bert and raised his eyebrows a little, then turned and went in the other direction.

Miriam opened the door of her room and ushered her visitors inside. She threw back the covers of the white bed and Bert placed Estelle inside it. She was unconscious now, a thin thread of dried blood running from a nasty cut in her head.

Miriam's face was white with grief and strain. The doctor turned his head and looked up at her. 'There's nothing you can do for your father anymore,' he said gently. 'Perhaps you'd like to help me here.'

The girl was dry-eyed. 'I should just have liked to have been with him at the last moment,' she said.

'I think he knew where you'd gone,' said Doc.

'That was the way he would've wanted it.'

Bert meandered over to the other side of the room while Miriam helped the doctor to strip some of the finery from Estelle. Except for her boots she had hardly been dressed for riding. Bert had not spotted a horse anywhere near the corral. Had the beast thrown her and bolted, or was there some other reason for the state she was in? How had she gotten to the Grosvenor place, anyway?

He heard the doctor say: 'She's kind of mussed up and shocked, but there aren't any bones broken and I don't think there are any internal injuries either. How did you come to pick her up?'

Miriam told him. He made no comment.

Estelle moaned. Bert forced himself not to turn his head. 'Hold this,' said the doctor, and Bert heard the clink of glass, the gurgling of liquid. Estelle made another little mewing cry and then was silent.

'Can you get me some hot water and towels?'

'Certainly.' Miriam crossed the room. The door opened, then was closed behind her.

Bert did not turn his head. 'Doc,' he said. 'What did old Grosvenor say before he died?'

'It's all written down, son.'

No more words passed between them. Bert picked up a vase from the mantelpiece, inspected it without seeing it, put it down again. The atmosphere of this place, the waiting, was beginning to get on his nerves. An old man dead along the passage, unspeaking. And in here a young girl lying, unspeaking too. And maybe both of them could have told him so much right now, when he most wanted to hear it.

Miriam returned with the water and towels and joined the doctor once more at the bed. Then after a while the latter said: 'She'll sleep now. We better go. Leave the light on.'

Bert followed the two of them from the room and along the passage to the room where the old man had died.

He admired Miriam's courage and poise as she lifted the white sheet and took one last look at the calm, dead face.

'Lawyer Cloony should've been here,' said the doctor. 'I'll go get him.'

He bustled off, but returned a few minutes later with the cadaverous lawyer in tow. Perry Cloony nodded at Bert, his poker face giving nothing away. He was about to shut the door when the shrill cry startled them all. It came from the room along the passage, a terrified voice calling Bert's name.

'It's all right,' said Bert. 'She's woken in a strange place an' is just scared, I guess. I'll go see to her.'

'That was a pretty strong sedative I gave her,' said Doc Mackey, making for the door. 'I can't under-stand—'

Bert forestalled him. 'I better go alone, doc. She knows me, I can calm her down.'

The doctor drew back, though a little uncertainly. Bert opened the door, went through it, closed it behind him. He wondered what effect his words and actions would have on Miriam. But he felt he had to see Estelle alone, though he wasn't quite sure why he wanted to do that.

As he halted at her door he heard the patter of her

133

feet inside the room. Then he opened the door and she gave a little scream and backed away from him.

'It's me, Estelle. Bert!'

But she had recognized him now and came back, almost knocking him over, so that he had to hold her, sooth her. Her slim body trembled in the flimsy things she wore. She was sobbing a little with relief and pleasure.

'You're all right now,' he assured her. 'You'll be quite safe here.'

'Yes, I remember now. I know where I am now. But what are you doing here?'

'Just visiting, I guess.'

'I don't understand. Are – are you working against Con, after all? Are you some kind of lawman – under-cover man or something?'

'It's a long story. Too long and complicated to tell you right now. I'd like you to tell me first of all what happened to you. Let's get you back into bed first, though, before you catch your death of cold.' He led her across the room, helped her to climb into bed, tucked her in.

'How d'yuh feel?'

'Better, thanks. A bit drowsy. But I feel like talking now. I want to talk.'

'Who did that to you? Con?'

'In a way, yes. He made me pack up tonight and ride out with him—'

'I know. Lenny the wrangler saw you go.'

'He didn't tell me what he meant to do. He didn't talk for a long time, keeping me guessing, torturing me. Then suddenly he started to tell me about what

134

he intended to do – but about you, not me.'

She paused, a little breathless. Bert poured her a glass of water from the carafe on the bedside cabinet and she sipped it before continuing:

'He's a devil, Bert. You don't know him – not really. He's a law unto himself. He doesn't believe anybody should go against him in any way. He's got more pride than a woman. He's mad with pride. You hurt his pride. He thinks you went behind his back, although I told him it was all my fault. In any case, he couldn't bear the thought that I preferred you to him. He's malicious and murderous. Although you've been very useful to him, he couldn't stack that up against his damned pride. He said you had to die. He had a nice plan all worked out. He was going to tell me all about it. What he meant to do with me when he had told it, I don't know.'

Estelle paused in order to sip some more water. The house was very silent. From outside came the mournful soughing of the wind. Bert wondered what was happening along the passage in the room with the dead old man, what the three living people there were saying, thinking.

The golden-haired girl went on: 'He means to attack the Caldicott Ranch in the early morning while it is still dark. He planned to let you ride in the forefront because you know the territory best, then when the battle is on to shoot you in the leg or some-thing and leave you to the tender mercies of the people in the territory. He figures they'd make a better job of you if they had a second chance. He hates this territory, these ranchers. He always has done; he'd like to take over this territory too, be king of it all. You don't know what he's really like, Bert. He's crazy – crazy!'

Estelle was becoming a little incoherent. The strain was beginning to tell on her again. Her blonde head was beginning to droop. She tried to lift it, her eyes seeking his appealingly. He admired her guts. She was a strange mixture.

'Take it easy,' he said. 'Slow!' He knew she had not finished yet. He must not let her rest until she had finished.

'What did he try to do to you?' he asked. 'How did you get away from him?'

'He had finished his tale and I knew there was something in store for me then; there was something devilish in his mind. Maybe he meant to shoot me in the leg too and take my horse away from me and leave me out on the plains to die. I daresay he figured he had me completely in his power, that he could do just what he wanted with me and I wouldn't be able to do a thing about it. So I caught him unawares – I hit him across the face with the butt of my quirt and knocked him from his horse. Then I ran. I meant to get to the Caldicott Ranch and warn them, but this isn't it, is it? So I must've gone in the wrong direction. After I had warned them I wanted to go back to Billstown and warn you. I thought maybe men from the ranch would ride with me – help me. I was riding towards this place when my horse caught its foot in a gopher-hole and threw me. He bolted. I managed to get as far as the corral. I was dazed, I must've mistook the corral gate for some-

136

thing else. The next thing I can remember is you coming towards me – the other side of the fence. Kind of significant maybe.' She gave a little hysterical giggle.

'You've got me wrong,' put in Bert. 'I don't think there's anything significant at all.' He became suddenly brisk. 'You don't have to worry about anything anymore. Just lie back now, try to go to sleep again.'

What she might have read into his words he did not know. Anyway, she did as she was told, and a few moments later was breathing gently and peacefully, her eyes closed. He stole from the room. Miriam was just coming through the door along the passage.

'Is she all right?' she asked.

Bert nodded. There was no suspicion in Miriam's manner, had been no rancour in her tone. But Bert had been with Estelle longer than he had bargained for and he figured maybe a little explanation was needed.

'She awoke, startled, wondering where she was. She's had quite a nasty experience. She had quite a story to tell me. Now she's got it all off her chest, she's sleeping peacefully. She'll be all right.'

'There's another story waiting for you in here,' said Miriam. 'Mr Cloony's getting kind of impatient.'

'What's Lawyer Cloony to do with me?'

'I expect Mr Cloony will tell you that himself.'

The lawyer was indeed in quite a sweat. It seemed he had promised his wife he would be home pretty early. Bert remembered his wife, a real ornery old battleaxe, and could not suppress a smile. Time was, a poor lad among rich neighbours, he had been rather in awe of the dry-as-dust lawyer. But now he felt powerful, contemptuous. If there was more trickery on the way, well, he would be more than ready for it.

Why all the mystery – did this slick shyster think he was pulling the wool over anybody's eyes? Bert couldn't help feeling that he was still in the camp of enemies, but he had a sudden, reckless disregard for danger. Both camps were against him. He was alone. But he would keep on fighting. Con; Cloony; the old man on the bed, reaching out already from death; Caldicott; the whole damn' boiling lot of them.

He looked at Cloony. 'All right,' he said curtly. 'Start talking.'

But this particular story was still yet not destined to be told. Two shots sounded from somewhere inside the house. The four people in the dead man's room were caught in attitudes of suspended animation. Once more Bert Cave was the first to move.

'Estelle!' he said. He dashed to the door, flung it open.

He ran along the empty passage. His gun was in his hand when he opened the other door.

Estelle tottered towards him, then, before he could reach her, fell on her stomach. He took in the shattered window, the curtains flapping in the breeze. He bent and rolled the girl over. Her breast was dyed with crimson. Her eyes looked into his appealingly for the last time, then closed. Behind him he could hear the running footsteps of the others. He ran to the window, flung the sash up recklessly and climbed out. His feet hit the veranda with a thud.

A slug smacked into the wall a few yards to the right of him. The bushwhacker had fired wild, was running now. There was something familiar about the scurrying figure in the pale starlight. Con Bryer? Had he caught up with Estelle after all? Who else could it be?

Running was awkward on the baked uneven ground in high-heeled riding-boots. Bert paused, balanced himself, took a shot at the fleeing figure. It did not pause in its stride and he knew he had missed. The figure disappeared into the darkness. He heard the clatter of a horse's hoofs, which broke into a gallop and quickly faded. He paused again to get his bearings, then turned and ran to get his own horse from the side of the house.

As he mounted and set off in pursuit of the murderer, the ranch was breaking into noisy life, the sound growing behind him, then fading quickly. The wind whipped at his bare head, thudded in his ears. He could not see his quarry now, could not even hear him.

He slowed his horse a little. He cursed the wind, which had risen considerably. The night was darker too, the stars hidden by lowering clouds. There were faint sounds of pursuit behind him now, which confused things even further. But finally he thought he heard the faint thud of hoofbeats up ahead, and he urged his horse onwards. It was a fast beast, the very one that Miriam gave him on the trail the day he was driven away from Faro Creek. That seemed countless ages ago.

The beast had already done a lot of racing tonight and Bert had not had much time to look after it in its interval of rest. It responded nobly, however, its muscles moving beneath him as if they were oiled, speed incarnate.

The murderer had a good start. If it was Con – and who else could it be? – he had a fine horse too. Bert hit the trail and halted again, wondering whether his quarry had taken it or continued to race on across the range, taking his chance on gopher holes and the rest. Now he could hear no sound, either from in front or behind, except the blustering of the wind. He realized that, despite his horse's magnificent effort, he had lost his quarry.

He patted the silky neck. 'Never mind, old scout, we'll get the coyote some day.'

This mood quickly passed; savagely he pushed on, hoping maybe that luck or accident would deliver his quarry into his hands.

He heard hoofbeats behind him, swelling suddenly. He wheeled his horse as the riders came out of the darkness. He raised his hand. He saw the flash; his horse screamed, the sound rising above the gunfire. Bert felt himself falling. His head burst into a myriad fiery fragments. Then there was nothing but blackness.

CHAPTER 13

When he came round he was in the saddle once more. His arms were draped around the horse's neck, the familiar pungent sweaty smell was in his nostrils. An arm was around his shoulders, steadying him in the saddle. His head felt as if it was full of cottonwool. He lay until it began to clear a bit. Then the arm across his shoulders, firm, holding him down, began to irritate. He jerked upwards savagely.

The arm was thrown away. The night spun around him, his head seemed to open again like a screaming mouth. He grabbed the horse's mane to steady himself. A hand grabbed his arm this time. A well-known voice spoke his name. He managed to find the reins. He held on to them, forced himself to stay upright in the saddle as he turned his head towards the apparition at his side.

'Miriam! What's going on?'

'One of our men shot at you by mistake. You waved to them. One of them thought you had a gun in your hand, so he threw down on you. You weren't hit but you fell on your head.

'I sure did.'

Bert suddenly realized that this spavined freak he rode was certainly not his own mount.

'Where's my horse?'

'I'm sorry, Bert, he's dead. He stopped the slug. It was quick. It's sad – he was a beautiful beast.'

'He was yours originally.'

'Yes, I know,' said Miriam, adding bitterly: 'I suppose it should be right that I – or, at least, one of my men should be the one to kill him.'

'You shouldn't talk like that. I guess it was just as much my fault, waving my arm about in the dark like I did – it was enough to start anybody shooting. I'll sure miss that hoss though.' Then, hoping to josh Miriam out of her gloom, he added: 'He always reminded me of you.'

'I'm not sure whether that's a compliment or not.' Her voice was brighter. He reckoned he couldn't expect her to be actually laughing her head off, anyway, not with her father lying dead. He kept forgetting about old Grosvenor, which wasn't surprising really, considering the fact that the landowner had tried to bury a hatchet in his skull a couple of times of late.

Thinking of Cal Grosvenor made him think of Jim Caldicott too. In his mind lately the two hated names had been almost interchangeable. And the latter was still among the land of the living. Bert couldn't help feeling it would have been much better had Caldicott been killed rather than Grosvenor – for his (Bert's) sake as well as Miriam's.

Still, if the Billstown mob were going to raid Caldicott's spread tonight, maybe the mighty Jim would get what was coming to him, after all.

Miriam broke into his train of thought. 'Who was the man?'

'I didn't get a good look at him, but I think it was Con Bryer. He had been chasing the girl.'

And if it was Con Bryer and he was on his way home again would he still insist on raiding the Caldicott Ranch in the early morning? Did he know that Bert Cave, the Kid, was at the Grosvenor place and, to double-cross him, might give the alarm to the whole territory? With the Kid gone, the boss wouldn't be able to carry out his subtle little plan of vengeance; but knowing Con, the Kid didn't think that fact would prevent the raid from coming off. The Kid didn't think Con had spotted him at the Grosvenor Ranch; or wouldn't the boss have bushwhacked the Kid as well as Estelle? Unless Con, when he had been running away, had recognized the Kid against the light of the window.

What was he worrying about, anyway? Bert asked himself. As far as he was concerned, the Bryer gang could blow Jim Caldicott and his mob to hell and gone if they wanted to.

The riders were a silent, sullen lot. Maybe if their young employer hadn't been present they would've wanted to stretch Bert Cave's neck again.

The ranch was reached.

Lawyer Percy Cloony was still waiting.

So was Doc Mackey. They had moved their quarters now though. Miriam and Bert joined them in the lounge. The two elderly men were both deeply sorry about the death of the girl. Bert smiled thinly, humourlessly. No platitudes could help Estelle now. Platitudes had never suited her; they wouldn't suit her now. Poor kid, she hadn't had much of a chance.

'Well, Mr Cave, perhaps now we can get down to business,' said Lawyer Cloony.

Bert had never been called 'Mr Cave' by a lawyer before, or by anybody else, if it came to that. His cynical smile widened a little. He sat down. 'Shoot,' he said.

They were all seated now in a semi-circle by the empty firegrate. The lawyer had the table near his elbow, and on the corner of the table, within his reach, was a sheaf of papers. The lawyer coughed primly and crossed his legs in their pinstripe pants and unadorned riding-boots. He addressed himself directly to the young man, the outlaw, the Kid.

'Cal Grosvenor would have liked to have seen you before he died, but that was not possible. He held on, he literally kept himself alive as long as he could, but his wounds proved too much for him.'

Spoken in dry lawyer's tones there was an added poignancy behind the words. Bert heard the girl next to him sigh. And the lawyer was still talking, telling it in his own way, passing on all that Cal had told him. It was a strange story, yet a credible one. Bert believed it, in parts he was overjoyed to believe. In other parts he could not believe his ears; but ultimately he was forced to believe them.

In the beginning Cal Grosvenor had thought his old friend, Jonathon Cave, was guilty of the murder

of Melody Jinks, guilty of the stealing of his neighbour's beef. The evidence was so overwhelming. But
after rangeland justice had been done – rangeland
justice at its worst – and he hadn't lifted a finger to
prevent it, he began to have doubts, twinges of
conscience. He looked into his heart.

Maybe he had wanted Jonathon to be guilty: the
thought appalled him.

Jonathon's property had been confiscated, osten-
sibly by the 'law' of Faro Creek. Then Jim Caldicott
came to Cal like a conspirator and offered to split the
Cave spread between them. It was small, but rich in
water. They had both coveted it for a long time.

Cal had put Jim off and the latter had cursed him
for a weak hypocrite. Then came the Bryer raid and
the identification of Bert Cave as one of the raiders.
This was followed shortly afterwards by the capture of
Bert Cave; and Cal veered once more to the popular
belief: like father, like son. Again the evidence was
overwhelming.

But Miriam's intervention, saving Bert's life, her
staunch defence of him, made Cal have doubt again.
He loved his only daughter above anything; he
admired her good sense. She had admitted that she
loved this young man, her childhood sweetheart. Cal
was getting old. He vacillated. Then by a stroke of
chance his mind was suddenly made up for him.

Some Grosvenor riders caught two of Jim
Caldicott's men using a running-iron on Grosvenor
beef. There had always been rivalry between the
punchers of the two big ranches; now it flared into
hate. The Grosvenor boys set about stringing up the

two cattle thieves right there and then. To save their own lives the two men spilled their guts about the whole cunning set-up of which Jim Caldicott and all his older and more trusted hands were a part. It was Jim's ambition to have all the range around Faro Creek. Jonathon Cave had been just a little 'victim'; now Jim was aiming for bigger game. The murder of Melody Jinks and the cattle-stealing on that fateful night had been done by some of Caldicott's men. Jonathon Cave had been framed.

The two Caldicott men had been brought back to Cal Grosvenor and had told him their story. And they had stuck to it.

'Those two men are still here,' said Lawyer Cloony. 'In the bunkhouse under guard.'

CHAPTER 14

Cal Grosvenor knew his friend Jim was an old rogue, but he could not believe that Jim could be guilty of such double-dyed villainy: he thought the two thieves were spinning a yarn or, at the most, exaggerating one, in order to save their own skins. Probably they had been doing a little rustling on the side, feathering their own nests. He hadn't told any of his men, or even his daughter, of his intentions, but he must have gone alone to talk this thing over with his old friend, Jim.

At dusk he was found by two of his own riders on his own land, shot to ribbons. He had been bushwhacked, had not even gotten a glance at his attacker. There was no clue.

'It was pretty obvious who was behind the shooting, wasn't it?' said Bert Cave. 'What are the men here, yellow skunks! Why didn't they ride on the Caldicott place, smoke the skunks out?'

'Cal wouldn't allow that,' said Lawyer Cloony. 'He was a man of peace who, for once, had made a mistake and become a man of violence. He couldn't forget how your father had been killed and that he might've been able to have stopped it. He couldn't forget how he had almost caused you yourself to be lynched. He didn't want to make another terrible mistake, start a range war perhaps. He wanted the law in on this. So on behalf of him I sent a wire to Ranger headquarters. Those people work fast; they're probably on their way right now.'

Perry Cloony looked about him. 'There remains only one more duty to perform on behalf of my old friend Cal,' he went on. 'Before he died he made a new will. I know that, though he hasn't been dead long, he would want me to tell you the contents of this will, so although this is highly irregular I intend to do so. He meant to tell you, Bert, part of this himself, but unfortunately that became impossible.'

Bert looked a little mystified, but said nothing. A hand came into view on the table near to him, Miriam's hand. Almost automatically he placed his own brown and sinewy hand atop of it. He turned and looked at her. She smiled tenderly, gave him a reassuring nod. It was as if she already knew, or had guessed, what the will contained.

Lawyer Cloony raised another sheet of paper from the table, cleared his throat, adjusted his pince-nez more comfortably. Then suddenly he put the paper on the table, settled himself more comfortably into his chair and clasped his hands together. Then he was looking at the two young people directly, looking at them over the top of his pince nez, which seemed to have slipped again.

'You don't want to listen to that dry legal phraseology. The actual conditions are very similar. The top and bottom of it is that Cal made one change. Whereas first of all he wanted to leave everything he owned to his daughter, Miriam, before he died, he changed his mind and decided to split everything into two parts, equal shares of everything between his daughter and Bert Cave, son of his old friend, Jonathon, whom he had wronged so terribly—'

Bert gasped. The lawyer did not give him chance to speak, but went on: 'Cal said that he could never make adequate reparation to you, Bert, for the death of your father, but he hoped this gesture would help to compensate a little. He thought that the two part-ners would work well together. He thought it was a good idea—'

Perry Cloony paused again. Then he added rogu-ishly, his eyes glinting behind his spectacles: 'I think it's a good idea myself. He couldn't have thought of a better one.'

Bert wondered why he had ever thought the lawyer to be a dry-as-dust old cuss. Miriam's fingers enveigled their way into his, closed around them. She said: 'You better let me have another look at that head of yours.'

He grinned. 'Yeah, it is aching again. Shock, I guess.'

Bert was given a spare room in the ranch-house. His brain was weary and there was a lump on his head as big as a duck egg. There was so much he had to think about; yet he was too tired to think. He struggled out of his clothes and threw himself into the bed like a log. In a few seconds he was fast asleep.

His subconscious mind would not let him over-sleep. When he awoke, the room was still dusky, but he could see through the windows that dawn was pearling the sky.

For a moment he thought he was back in the room in Billstown.

He felt under his pillow for his gun. It was not there. In the dim light he spotted his gunbelt hanging over the back of a chair nearby, the gun intact. He reached for it idly and spun the chambers. They were full. He remembered refilling them automatically last night, after doing the last of his shooting. The events of last night came back to him then. The good things and the bad things; the good ones predominating. Things had seemed like a nightmare; then suddenly – as if a medicine-man had waved a magic stick – they had become like a roseate dream. But as he got out of bed now and padded across to the window and looked out, he knew that these things were true.

The dawning Western sky was streaked with all the hues of a rainbow. Through the window Bert could see the local range of small mountains, their tops hidden by a soft purple haze through which the sun was already beginning to break. And, lower down, the magical colours chased themselves across the rangeland grass, shimmering in the breeze.

A new day; and the promise of a good day. The promise of a new life, a good life for Bert Cave – with the guns of hate stilled forever. But there was much to do yet.

He turned away from the window and went over to the washstand and laved his face, neck and arms vigorously. He massaged his scalp gingerly. The lump had gone down, but was still a little sore. He dressed, put on his riding-boots, buckled on his gunbelt automatically. He picked up his battered hat and poked his finger ruefully through the hole in the crown, a hole put there by one of the dry-gulch merchants at the fork of the trail last night.

He wondered if the two bodies had been discovered and what the scheming Jim Caldicott thought of that. Still, Jim would have a hell of a lot more to think about soon: the Rangers would be paying him a visit. Bert went into the passage, closed his door gently behind him. The house was silent, probably everybody was still sleeping. But from the direction of the bunkhouse he heard sounds of life stirring. The old boss was dead, but the work had to go on. A new day, very much like countless ones gone before, was beginning for the cowpunchers.

Bert went out on to the front veranda and stood there with his makings, building himself a quirly. A man came away from the bunkhouse and crossed the yard, glanced in his direction, carried on. He passed from sight into the gloom of the barn. The sky was lightening, the soft colours were giving way in places to an almost metallic brightness. Suddenly there was a feeling in the air of something about to happen. Then Bert Cave heard the hoofbeats in the distance and he felt suddenly that, in the back of his mind, he had been waiting for them. His mood of complacency was shattered; he wondered if he had made

151

another mistake, a terrible mistake.

The two riders came into view through the golden haze. And then the sun was behind them and they were etched against it like black, cut-out carboard figures growing quickly larger. They were riding so close together that every now and then they looked like one figure, fantastically shaped.

Bert Cave recognized them. They were Jack Tremaine and Con Bryer. Jack was upright in the saddle, but Con was hunched up and wobbling all over the place. Jack had one hand stretched out and was holding his companion in the saddle.

As they drew abreast of the corral, Con slipped sideways. Jack tried to prevent him from falling, but he failed. Con pitched from the saddle and lay still. Jack dismounted and bent over Con, then straightened up slowly. He looped his horse's reins over the corral-rail, did the same with the reins of Con's mount. His movements were a little weary, but deliberate. He started to walk towards the ranch-house, his arms swinging loosely at his sides, a wizened young-old man with a limp.

Bert Cave went down the verandah steps. He didn't know whether Jack had seen him. He went out to meet him.

The man who had gone into the barn came suddenly into view from the gloom. The bunkhouse door opened and another man appeared. Both men had guns in their hands.

'Leave him be!' Bert Cave's voice rang out like a whiplash.

The two men's heads jerked around. Then, slowly,

both of them lowered their guns.

Jack Tremaine had paused, half-crouched, his arms suddenly bent. But now he came on again, making straight for Bert. He was looking at Bert, but there was no kindliness in his face, no expression at all.

His thin lips opened, his words rang out on the still air.

'I thought I'd find you here. Con said we would. I didn't believe him when he said you were a yellow, treacherous skunk. Not until we ran into the troop of Rangers you'd sent for to take care of us in case we got you a bad name or something.'

The words bit into Bert Cave's mind. He hadn't thought the Rangers would get to the territory this quickly.

'We ran into them on Caldicott's land, they knew we'd be there. Only one man could've told them. We were wiped out, all of us except me and Con—' Jack's voice cracked. 'Med, Grado, Candy, Tim Baggs, the man who saved your life – all of them gone. Now Con's gone. Con's no loss to you I know: he hated you, he thought you'd stolen his girl, he meant to kill you. He didn't tell me this until we were on our way here. If he had told me before I should've tried to stop him killing you – my friend.' Jack laughed harshly. 'Can you imagine that—?'

Bert found his voice. 'I didn't send for the Rangers, Jack. They—'

The rasping voice cut him short. 'Con's dead – the others – maybe they didn't mean anything to you even if they were your saddle-buddies. But Tim – and me! Why us? Goddamn you for a two-faced, treacherous, lily-livered cur.'

They were still walking very slowly, but drawing steadily closer to each other. Bert could see Jack's face clearly, the eyes cold, abysmal – killer's eyes. He remembered how Jack himself had always told him to watch the other man's eyes. But now Jack was his opponent: the thing hit him like a blow in the stomach! It must not be!

'You got to listen to me, Jack. I wouldn't do that to you. You know me better than that. Hold on a bit. I–'

It was like shouting into a storm. 'I've got nothing more to say,' said Jack. 'I've only got one thing to do. I'm calling you out, you skunk. I taught you to shoot. Let's see how good you are. Maybe you're even good enough to beat me.'

Bert realized Jack didn't bother about himself anymore. He knew that if he killed Bert he wouldn't leave this ranch alive. He knew he was finished, but that didn't matter any more: he'd go out as every gunfighter should. But he'd go out thinking the young man he had befriended had betrayed him. That was the cruellest death of all!

They were very close now. Jack was falling into a crouch. He wasn't talking anymore. Bert didn't try to talk either. He knew it was useless. He was taller than Jack. He could have reached out and touched his friend.

He moved swiftly forward. His feet went slap-slap in the dust, his fist looped out like a weight on a string and sank into Jack's middle, doubling him up.

154

The other fist described an arc.

The second blow exploded on the side of Jack's jaw. His gun, brought out of its holster by the fastest draw in the West, flew in the air, hit the ground with a flat sound a few yards away. Jack hit the ground with his side, and rolled. Bert drew his own gun. When Jack straightened into a sitting position he saw Bert resting on one knee in front of him, pointing a gun at his head.

'Keep still an' listen, or I'll blow a hole in you, anyway.'

'Don't waste your breath,' sneered Jack. 'Go ahead and shoot.'

'I didn't send for the Rangers. They were sent for by Cal Grosvenor before he died. He had been bush-whacked, probably by one of Jim Caldicott's men. Caldicott's been double-crossing everybody in the territory for years. I never dreamed the Rangers would be that quick. You didn't meet them at Caldicott's place, did you?'

'No. We met Caldicott's bunch first. They were out riding. We thought they had been warned too. You—'

'They were probably on their way here to finish the job they'd started with the dry-gulching of Cal Grosvenor.'

'Jim Caldicott's dead and his son. And his boys scattered to hell an' gone. But we had casualties too; we had to turn back. Then we ran smack-dab into the Rangers.' Jack's lips quirked mirthlessly. 'They're on my tail now. I'm finished!'

'No.' Bert shook his head vigorously. A shadow fell

across them and he looked up and saw Miriam standing there. There was the light of understanding in her eyes.

She turned her head. Her voice rang out. 'Get a fresh horse, the fastest we've got. And plenty of chow and water, and a bedroll.'

Her voice was decisive, authoratitive. Men ran to do her bidding. Bert helped Jack to his feet.

'I should've known,' said Jack softly. 'I'm sorry, pardner.'

'Forget it. An' you'll be back – that's something you must not forget. We'll be waiting for you here.'

The horse was brought and all the necessary things. Jack Tremaine mounted it. Bert Cave handed him his gun and, ruefully, he pouched it.

His eyes had that kindly light again as he looked down at the two young people.

'Look after him, ma'am,' he said.

'I will.'

He rode at a gallop towards the border, turning on the crest of the rise to wave to them as they stood there side by side. Then he passed at last from their sight and they turned away from the past and walked hand in hand to the ranch-house and a new life.